QUERENCIA

SUMMER 2025

Querencia Press – Chicago Il

QUERENCIA PRESS
© Copyright 2025

ISBN

978 1 963943 48 1

www.querenciapress.com

First Published in 2025

**Querencia Press, LLC
Chicago IL**

Printed & Bound in the United States of America

CONTENTS

POETRY

Birthday Hymn

Cradled safely in pastel flowers
          And warm, swishing waterfalls
Lay the slumbering creature in the hours
          Of her rest before landfall

On the outside, they all fretted—
          Fussed and prayed and wept with awe
"O, great creature! What a blessing!"
          Shot of joy to cure their flaws

Steady beeping, sterile stretcher
          Unflattering lights galore
Silly creature glimpsed the outside
          Said, "No thank you," it's a bore

"Emergency!" White coats a-shuffle
          "Flip this critter back to fore!"
Then comes in the man to numb her
          Having numbed himself much more

SLICE!

          A guttural screech

BOOM!

          A burst through the door

BACK, YOU ANIMALS!

          Creature's maker sees the gore

SHE CAN FEEL EVERYTHING!

          Lolling in her cervicals
          Mother loses control
          The white coats send her
          On a rainbow kart road

Slipping, sliding, creature's cradle
        is safe no more
In come swirling the bright rainbows
        Taint the swishing waterfalls

Swim away! Creature, swim to safety
        Have your limbs become a stone?
Skilled hands and quick stitches
        Pull the creature violently forth
Place her, red and groggy on the mother—
        "We saved her!"
Scream aloud! Creature, tell them,
        "I never wanted to be born"

—CAROLINA MURRIEL (she/they)

The pill replaces want with hunger, trading one
slate of emptiness for another. The pill is an oblong

shape, an appealing blue, with a number written on
the side in black. The number changes as the days

change—first up, then down, then up again, shimmying
itself into a wave, the worm. I am not a worm on most

days, but every day I look I see a different symbol next
to the number. The pill looks at me and finds me wanting.

My blue is not appealing, not studied, not market-tested.
I Google names for the blue of the pill: cerulean,

hex #4fbaee, style="color:deepskyblue;". The blue is dynamic,
adept at disappearing deep into sky and riding carnival-style swings,

falling asleep on rollercoasters and seesaws, treating gravity
and kinetics as casual suggestions. The pill has been known to engage

in blue-sky thinking and scores highly on agreeableness and openness.
I am an ocean wave, an open maw, ravenous. I score, high

on conscientiousness and neuroticism. The pill looks
at me and finds me, wanting. I take azure assurances

and find I am well
within the bounds

of my body. When measured with calipers,
the shape of my skull is not oblong, but despite

our difference in architecture, the pill
tells me that we are within range

of usual operating parameters. I lack sufficient parameters
to run this optimization. My blue is too much green grass,

more of a teal. I confuse pharmacodynamics with
pharmacokinetics, but despite our difference in optimal measurement

criteria, I suspect the pill is taking effect. I take
the knife off the operating table and carve myself a bitc.

—**DEREK YEN** (he/him)

MIND FRAGMENTS

I.
My brain is changing color.
I refuse love like poison.
A wildcard of a person.

Of my earliest memories,
of the ones that stayed,
I am chewing the clothes
worn on my back.

II.
How does one quit self-sabotage?

An easy crier,
exhausted by hope.
My memories are made up of feelings,
survivor's guilt,
the black holes of their eyes
revolving around me.

We were artful youth,
polygons, polyglots.
But all of our dreams
are double-edged swords.

Once, in my glory days,
I was a nihilist.
But nothing belonged to me,
not even my sanity.

III.
Bury me in
all my abandoned hobbies.
A failed state of mind,
a conditional form.
Paralyzed.
Motionless.
Emotionless, too.

IV.
I weep now,
but only ever for joy.
The madwoman
that learned to outrun sorrow.

For artful youth,
peace did come in pieces.

The walls reek of petrichor.
Let me drown
in all this oxygen.

Bury me with
all my abandoned selves.

—Augustina Naanret Dasat (she/her)

Mama stomps the black cigar.
Mama hates an ordinary answer.
Our family ekes a new era.
Father was born in an author's wick.
My sister has hollowed hands.
I pin skins to a frame.
Mama burned my confession.

—CONNOR FISHER (he/him)

SUNDAY'S SPOILS

Lone drizzle. A crooked pathway down the
window. Tree lines gathering
silent sparrows. Waiting
without mourning
their sudden loss of light.
The entrance
of an early dusk.

Gripped again by
weak hands
dispositioning you. Half smiles without faces
in screenborne shadows appear
by the minute
on your wall. Familiar
ruptured tempo of things.
A quivering canyon
in the aftershocks of
something
unfelt.

You could take your frayed baseball cap and raincoat. You could go
outside. You could listen for the sparrows without the gluttony of
desiring their songs and commune with something. You could sing to
them—you could. You know the rhythm. You know these mealy hands
will ungrip and cradle you for fun so why don't you defy those moments?
Why don't you ever sanctify those moments? You could take them and
stretch your whole self into them without waiting for them to be given—
you *could*. Tear out of your throat the locked strands of hair it slow-drum
forced you to swallow one by one
with
out
retching.

A patient violence outlasts a whimmed burst
of guttural desire
by
its
nature.

It follows a credo. Inside you
it penned a manifesto. It
has a
check list. A cache
of recipes. An egg timer. It knows you
know it wants to slow-stir its whisk of
thorny rose stems
inside you as
soon as you inhale and reach
your hands to
heaven. When the storm recedes and the late sky's acolytes rekindle a
hazy sun and rain rinsed dirt releases mist from the road and you feel
yourself take that first deep breath of fresh earth because you can't push
it out or hold it back any longer and for a moment you forget—you *can*
forget this violence. Still crackles
imperceptibly

like the last
glowing ember that won't
burn out.

—STEPHANIE JONES (she/her)

WHOLE

If I am, it is hard
won.
Blue ribbon with a gold
anchor. Boat
polished by drift
and wind.
I've been pulled in.
Congratulate me
on docking in the ground-shell beach,
my necklaces of kelp
still pulsing in the leaving waves.

—JULIETTA BEKKER (she/they)

Hypnagogia

A mirrored figure haunts me,
lustrous limbs lost to tall pines
soaked in the moon's spilled whisky,
bare feet tangling with tree limbs,
waist-length hair a colorless exhale.
At this hour she is sleepwalking in a landscape my body knows
but hasn't stepped foot in for centuries.
She forages for a talisman no bigger than a morel,
which she'll shear with palmed light
to fasten around my neck. Once dried,
its roots can be soaked and applied
to clot night terrors.
Last night she was a woman, tonight
she is a silver cross fox stalking
a speckled hare along the edge of a black lake
filled with bottomless stars.
What she stalks, I become—
soft in her mouth
where the sharp points of her teeth
are a tender warning
to listen and abide by the laws of nature.
She consumes me, her bowels
a reflection of night stretched
to flesh and turned inside out.
We become a contraction of time, tomorrow
blotting the horizon with our mourning song,
dew heavy on the heads of far-reaching
graminoids as every grass blade morphs
into a throat reverberating,
carrying the vast recital
of what cannot be helped.

—SHELBY NEWSOM (she/her)

the comfort of a future

every headline
a new
reason to internally
scream,

every day
my country becomes more
of a joke;

and i can't laugh
or cry
about it any longer
because it's just what
life seems to be
these days—

all i want is the comfort
of a future,

when i was a child
they promised me a dream
without any intention of
giving it to me;

now i'd like a dream
where i can at least live.

—LINDA M. CRATE (she/her)

what it's like to exist as a woman right now

fingernails split clinging tight to change yanked again from clenched fingers
a mocking tide rushes horizon we strain four years eight years or rather
this side of never to reach i've got a big rusty knife in my belly the majority lines
up to twist oblivious to the worst case in my head now reality plaguing air we
breathe dawn does not flinch on brutality   a mouse in a glue trap trembles in
cold sweat bath because struggle does not change fate but blind faith in my sex
keeps me on the road to justice women have worn to asphalt crumbs   crawling
on all fours we push over thorns and nettles and salt and bleed from knees and
palms and cunt howling grief to waning moon   how many ways must we prove
we have value beyond our biology   for how long   unhinge my jaw eat bad
men crunch thick skulls savor toughness of talk-too-long tongues pick teeth with
accusing pointer finger bones   we approach our last shred of dignity   i'm awake
wondering if the State will come for me because i am rudely alive   the harm we
brew lives in throats chafed with rage

—MIRO (she/her)

24

BETHLEHEM

If I'm honest, the story reached me
like heat rolling in off desert stone
this man, not yet thirty,
pulling water from the bones of jars
and making it wine. They say he opened
a blind man's eyes with spit and dust,
called a dead man out of his tomb
like it was nothing more than sleep.
But what if, by some ruin in the stars,
some curse woven through our lineage
like cracked olive branches,
the grief still comes
no matter how we bow,
or lift our hands toward something greater?
The way they found Ezra's boy
folded in the straw behind the stable,
face calm as if dreaming,
the mother shaking him softly,
then not at all
what god would allow that?
Am I wrong to say I stopped praying after that?
I even said as much on the walk back
through the alleys of the old quarter,
where bread cost more than a man's word,
and word of miracles passed
quicker than famine.
Even now, when someone says
they've seen him—the Nazarene
standing in the market with eyes
like fire held at bay,
I feel my chest lock up.
At any moment, something terrible
could crack open again.
A child gone, a wife taken by fever.
The ache hasn't left me.
It sits behind the ribs,
quiet as a lion waiting.
They say he walks among us now.

That he weeps. That he laughs.
That his touch is like morning.
But I have been wrong before.
I have waited, and nothing came.
Still . . . still
I want it to be true.
I want the blind to see.
The dead to rise.
The stone rolled back.
One day, I will believe again,
I feel it coming—
like thunder under sand.
I will walk the path barefoot,
head bowed,
asking only for a sign
that the world might heal.
That someone still walks among us
who remembers how.

—RAIS TULUKA (he/him)

dead ends and deficits

i'd like to touch cornflowers and wild grass growing beyond this dead end
where water tastes like copper   and sharp edges snag my clothes

in a warmth deficit   tired hands clutch stray threads

i envy rock conceived in magma   frothing fluid alive
in total surrender   becoming bold undulating light and shadow

an open palm   knots rooting in tree trunks rather
than clenched shoulders holding how i really feel about the moment

counting deep breaths   free to stretch long
under stars waiting patient for me to let go of the grip i got

stiff is the neck that holds the head that wears the cynic's crown
a fake formed in lead   covered in flaking layers of pyrite

it is a serious thing to be alive it should not ache this much

—Miro (she/her)

TANGLED YARN

Our living room is familiar with noise
Mom and Dad screeching teakettles
so unlike where Bubby knits on my couch
Wednesday after 5th grade
wrinkly fingers like a caterpillar
        a soft click, click, clicking of metal needles
        knitting the garden like a scarf

Tangled memories
I can no longer hold inside
explode like crashing cymbals

Do you see how I wrap the yarn around the needle?   No. I swallow like a dark
                                          fish floating in the
                                          shadow of a pond

The soft click, click, clicking of needles stops

Don't you want to knit today?   No. I wind my fingers
                                          into a ball of yarn.

You kept on knitting   last week
        when I told dad that he was bad
You kept on knitting   last week
        when he knocked me to the floor
you kept on knitting   last week
        when I hit my head.

That night
Bubby gives me her needles with soft-green yarn and says,
Here let me show you:

You can control the yarn, she tells me,

        while a soft-click, clicking hums on and on,

even if you can't control anything else.

—LYNNE DOLLE (she/her)

RECYCLED SHATTERSONG

Phone lines thrive despite the migratory season,
a choir's call trafficking against my quartered heart.

Is it too much to ask for a lungful of sparrows?
Anonymity singing. Beaks phalanxing newly bare bushes.
Steadiness in the sweep and spill choreographing wings,
the scatter and resurgence a carousel feathered over hurt.

My breath is absorbed with flight
-lessness, wishbone broken by glass eyes in the grass
ready for threshing. But the scythe's song struck first,
mulched like so many leaves crackling unheard
below the mower's droning. It's unreasonable
laying blame at my doorstep, yet I bend and bow
to the bird's burning chest. A robin's resting heart rate triples
mine collapsing, which makes it hard to trust
this mirroring of swell and shallow
before its ashy head tucks into a leadened stare.

Stillness crisps the air without the sun's vibration.
Resistance creaks a pooper-scooper's spring
rusting in summer's disuse, appetite for the dregs of life
hinged to a reticent jaw. Double bagged and tied tight,
the trash can rings hollow, unwilling to cushion
dusk's thud with clouds or silence. The lid's fall offers a prayer
lost to the song lost canyoning through me, my pulse
knotted under plastic ribs, rotomolded bones pleading for the robin
to beat out from my pupils one last use of sky.

—STEVEN O. YOUNG JR. (he/him)

Q&A

I lop off a chunk of fingertip
too eager for introductions.
No handshake is forthcoming

    in this moment of exposed nerves
       you toss over your shoulder
          a train of Caribbean Duskywings
             butterflying through the doubt

you've seated front and center
before a lens you judge as sharp
as the smoky topaz of your eyes
glossing over the audience
strung out in archipelago.

What here gives you worry?
                We're all adrift at sea.

Find mooring in your voice,
flesh out the animals
under your tongue.
Their claws and songs will stake the earth
flagged for your be|long|ing.
              Why are we portioned
           to the wilds of our lonesomeness?

The world is movable
when lent your imagination,
every mountain a pyre
ignited by colliding breaths.
                Contrails overlap,
             but it's just the footprint
                of a lost ghost
             smothered by the next.

Do you sense a disconnect
between prescription and reality?
             Only with my eyes open.
                Or closed.
          Survival is shorthand for fuzzying
                  logic.

Lion's teeth form
from the softest cotton.
Weathering shape to shape
is more art than imitation.

          Time's bludgeoning swing
          freewheels without design.
          How much do you trust
          the gravity of another's arms?

I abide each law
the universe has sworn to protect me.
          Strange. Physics reduces
          all the ways to pull me down
          to a science.

Even after everything comes crashing,
our world is nothing
but potential.

          How do you
     dread   dream
        so freely?

What separates us	I trudge through the ruins
isn't a difference in thought.	that lie before me
I find myself	with sunlight at my back.
aligned with you,	Denial lifts no burden
and that's where I take hope.	while bright eyes
Gloom is edacious	lighten the load.
for our disaster,	My legs may want to give,
but you thrash the dark	but you stand
elements grasping at your heart.	braced for every fall.

        Sitting here
       across from you
makes believing a relief.   makes relief believable.

—STEVEN O. YOUNG JR. (he/him)

On Learning the City of San Antonio is Phasing Out the Horse-Drawn Carriages Downtown

Blinders have I, too—
ignorant of the fumes from car exhaust
that cling around their muzzles,
waft into large nostrils.
Or the three-digit heat that turns
the asphalt on which steel horseshoes step
into stoves. If only
I could undo the rides I've taken
in these quaint carriages
to which these lovely creatures
were harnessed, never
thinking they might be hurting.
Or dreaming of cool weather,
open fields, gallops without reins.
Oh, the turns we made
on Market Street, Main Plaza,
Houston, South Alamo.
The turn I've made now, years in the making,
route harder yet unbridled.

—JONATHAN FLETCHER (he/him)

CONDOMS AND CROWS

sea blushes—
confessions of Digha's beaches
after Holi:
color-streaked rubbers
washed ashore—
saltwater cringes

crow perches on rusted lamp—
a failed open-mic at Gariahat:
"soft-lard mortals," it caws,
"I've eaten scraps of gods,
seen their plastic desires."

blindfolded crowbar
leans against locked heart:
unlock me, it whispers—
steel ribs shiver
like a lover caught
at Snakes & Ladders

past wheat fields—
cherry trees fake bloom,
pipes giggle in frolic,
locksmith reels
from imaginary whale

sunset hovers—
an ex who won't leave
the group chat

crow remains—
eye bound by truth:
condoms. crowbars. chaos.

sea carries everything.

—SABYASACHI ROY (he/him)

A MAN'S HEAD FLOATS some inches above his shoulders. His left ear is missing; in its place, a handle. He tips his head forward and its contents spill out his mouth's spout. But now the contents of a man's head are spilled all over the floor, like marbles. Yes, a man has spilled his marbles all over the ground, so that if one is not careful he might slip and fall; so to row about the contents of a man's head spilled haphazardly about. And here a centaur toots his conch shell horn; and here a mousetrap. And now one has stubbed his toe in the eye socket of a porcelain doll . . .

Across the vacancy of a man's head drifts a rolling plain of clouds.

—JUSTIN HOLLIS (he/him)

Still Life with Lemons

The lemons are shriveled
but bright—
nearly glowing,
just not as they once did.

I won't throw them out yet.

I said I was fine
but the dryer stopped
and I didn't move.

I sat
while the clothes cooled—
creasing slowly under their own weight,
staying warm longer than you'd think,
submitting to their current shapes.

Someone taped a reminder
to the door from the kitchen to the garage—
arrive by 5:30, east entrance.
I left it there
just to see how long the tape would hold.

I wish I had something
new
to want.

But all I want
still
is reversal
or resurrection.

So I keep the lemons
until they collapse
plump stars,
then rocks,
asteroids.

The sky wasn't anything.
But still,
I looked up.

—Dara Laine (she/her)

WHAT MOTHER TAUGHT ME

1.

In summer I'd chase down the
last of the mock orange blooms

fill sweaty palms with fallen
petals, offer them to the sky—

breathe
    the sun.

2.

Splayed like a starfish in the
shade of knotted California Bays

I make friend of stillness—watch the ground
squirrels work with frightening intensity

no acorn or black walnut left unforaged
even tender buckthorn is stripped of bitter berries

under chittering scurry, a storm of fur and paws
a gale force lesson in efficiency, in preparation.

3.

On my worst days when I am more
lost than I am my self

I wade into the river, wash from my arms the
sweat that clings to me like needy child

try to come clean to murky water,
instead, sob in ripple-causing shudders

when my toes sink into the muck—
how nice it is to be held.

I think about the fish—
the fish I can not see, but know are there—

I've never once doubted the bass or catfish—never
questioned the unwavering persistence of sturgeon

and maybe
that is
faith too.

—KONRAD EHRESMAN (he/him)

No Meaning

Boundless kindness is like the bad smell
of something gone wrong in the middle.
Hope raised by easy virtue falsely told
like spring's first bud, when
snow snoozes in repose, wind gathering
like a hockey team around the puck
to blow ice in brutal attack,
and we, deceived by unchecked belief
are slayed as truth unfolds.
We bleed from lies revealed,
and lucky, learn how deep a dagger cuts
in words easily said, but with no meaning.

—Ann Grogan (she/her)
The italicized line comes from D.H. Lawrence, "The Evening Land"

shawl and pickle

the shawl folds itself
          without help now—
    muscle memory
          from a hand
    that forgot
    how to weave.

  its edges:
    frayed
          borders
              drawn too fast.

      the threads smell
          of
    mustard oil
          and
    afternoons
          spent
          under
            ceiling fans.

    a jar in the cupboard
        chilli mango pickle—
        the oil
              bleeds
        through
            wax paper,
      a language
          I was meant
              to forget.

      I try it on
            too warm
                for London
            but
                not warm
                    enough.

a thread
   dangles
      like a sentence
      she
         never
            finished.

—SOMRWITA GUHA (she/her)

YOU WILL LIVE WONDERING

You turn 21, and your father rolls you a joint. Thick, scarred fingers make it messy work. Too-stuffed, bent left. He takes one hit and you take the rest. Then, the dizziness. Then, the couch. He wants to throw the frisbee, you want to lie down. Maybe this is the place where The Mistake was made.

But, you cannot know.

And, you cannot know that it was his own hand, until days later, in a restaurant with his mother and sister. "I didn't realize he was hurting so badly." Oh, oh. You had wondered. Guessed: car crash, altercation, something unavoidable and unpredictable.

You are served a plate of something you do not see.

—NAUDIA REEVES (she/her)

The Fundamental Laws of Nearly Everything

I. Physics of Absence
reaction ↔ nothingness
coffee cools at 9.8 m/s²—
touch lost to gravity

entropy stirs the spoon
quiet vandal in sugar

solve for x in us→
equation crumbles
ghost in denominator

voice becomes spectral wave
heard but unseen
Doppler-shifted farewell

mornings measured
in half-lives of glances

hawk circles backyard
waiting—carrion or miracle

wind mocks:
calculus of chaos
variables = loneliness

I scribble on existence's griddle
watch pancakes brown
poems bubble into void

II. March Algebra
loneliness = ?

divide self by horizon
wind rattles equations
inequality of warmth

sunset ≠ solace
clouds graph uncertainty
curves toward gray infinity

wind has teeth
feeds on fractions
skin cracks—solve for blood

shadow splits:
numerator above
denominator below

night falls as proof
I remain theorem unproved

III. Birdsong in Binary
01110100 01101000 01100101

birds—or static?
forgot how to listen
beyond screens

dreamt of robins→
now track coordinates
extinction rates

wings = algorithms
flight paths mapped
too straight for wonder

I envy chaos
analogue whispers
feathers pulse
against deaf sky

IV. Chemical Hearts

love = reaction gone wrong

C_2H_5OH floods my veins
molotov memory

your laughter combusts
ashes of affection

we burned exothermic—
too bright for balance

you NaCl · me H_2O
dissolved into nothingness

I breathe molecules you left
unstable isotope of dreams

V. The Sadness Algorithm

input: breath · thought · desire
output: machine too human

1. subtract joy; multiply despair; silence gallery
2. sex = glitch; parabola ‖ asymptote
3. nobody changes; rivers flow backward

final output: life simulation
pixels flicker
screen too dim to care

—SABYASACHI ROY (he/him)

Devoutly Cryptic

I take amusement in the known-as fact
That a never-ending soiree of pronouns
Will be used to confuse onlookers
Of my last ghastly presence, as if
I were a god.

Me,
A licensed atheist.

—Taylor Kovach (they/them)

WARNING: The Daffodils

WARNING: The daffodils are blooming too early. My little brother asked what my pronouns are. The paint is chipping off my boots. We're learning the names of new animals and repeating them every week. WARNING: The computer is 95% sure that bird is a person. I can hear the love of my life humming through the wall. Someone needs to tell the daffodils to go back to sleep. It's not even March. WARNING: Sometimes I am lying. Everything is in a particular order. My brother never asked my pronouns; he asked me about someone else's. It's a start. WARMING: Sometimes I am doing the wrong thing on purpose. It's not always a cry for help. WARNING: There's blood on the pavement. Watch out for falling birdhouses. Watch out for mixed metaphors. Misused vocabulary. WARNING: Don't follow me. I hardly ever know my point until it arrives. WARNING: 95% of the paint on my boots is flawless. Guess which parts I look at. WARNING: Sustained, repeated urgency loses its impact. WARNING: Sometimes I am not lying. Sometimes I mean it.

—SKYLER WITHERSPOON (they/them)

summer vacation blues

when days grow longer
melancholy comes
in swathes of warmth
distorted midday
d i z z y n e s s

the memory
of loneliness
clings to
my melting bones
is the sweat from heat
or anxiety?

i never quite know
did i ever hate summer
or did i just
hate my teen
y e a r s
dragged out
too l o n g
despite my
chronic
death wish?

sunlight should be
a sublime sight
but is it really?
not when heat-hazy
hope and
l o n g i n g
take me back
to wavering asphalt
free time
subtle gut-punch
glares
empty
poetry album

pages
ink not smeared
where it was
meant to be

seasonal sadness
in sunscreen silence
and timed trauma
traded for teenage turmoil

that's what i get
instead of vacation—
the price i pay
for learning too early
how to drown
u n n o t i c e d
and wash myself up
on the same old shore
weeks later
every year
in endless
l o o p s

—IRINA VÉRÈNE (they/them)
First published in Margins Mag

listening to mitski in the MRI (machine-body interfaces)

i sit where you sat ten months earlier. a gestation. you have never been in this room before /
entering the cave again / shadows on plato's white wall / an ideal form / that is, a body / you
stared ahead / i stare at black-worn-down-to-grey shoes / gaze into machine / machine
echoes itself a resonance machine heart machine brain machine spinal cord / dark circle
above surrounded by white black white grey / everything is clear

nothing is clear / air sings, needles its way inside again / a needle sends frost through veins. I
hold a tree, finger its needles. last time snow lit on tree branches / crimson verdant wiring
streetlights, salt sweet on tongue / *a whole cake* / yellow fans flutter in silence, autumnal
ghost ready to flip turn over / emerging from pool a body of water becomes a fluorescence
retinal burn of leaping dogs / blinking eyes into reality hard to tell whether you were more
ghost inside the machine or out

struggling / bookstore shelves a labyrinth you circled / sought same names different
bestsellers / i can forgive the unsubtle angst of *my body's made of crushed little stars* for the
title alone / you too embodied unspent teenage angst once / circling centripetal force of a
mosh pit in san diego / orbiting unknown celestial bodies / time is made of circular paths

& when mitski sings nobody / no / body / no / i cannot help but hear double negation
insistence upon a star / a body / all of its complications / indications / subtle signals / ghosts /
immaterial ambiguations

if as sontag suggested / the body is more than metaphor / if as johanna hedva said / *my
body is a prison of pain so i want to leave it like a mystic but i also love it & want it to matter
politically* / where is my body now, if not strapped down / plugged in / powered on / within
the machine / my body is not a prison but it is american / hedva again: the body as anything
that needs support / i ask the machine to love me

you didn't expect an answer / you were not born in this country / your best american self:

—DEREK YEN (he/him)

**contains referencesto several songs by the artist Mitski, including "Washing Machine Heart," "I Don't
Like My Mind," "Your Best American Girl," "Nobody," and "My Body's Made of Crushed Little Stars".
Italicized phrases are direct quotes of lyrics or titles. also referenced Susan Sontag's work "Illness as
Metaphor," and the name of Johanna Hedva's lecture titled "My Body Is a Prison of Pain so I Want to
Leave It Like a Mystic But I Also Love It & Want It to Matter Politically."*

listening to mitski in the MRI (machine-graded examinations)

i spot our landlord's office on the way to the machine
think about walking in to negotiate, but it's already late
somewhere in a room law and order is playing
you know the one, the episode with the cops

a child cries while chairs laugh, fingers clacking on keys
let my machine brain stay attached to my machine spinal cord
if i am the one in the machine, then who is the ghost?
is it me? my certainty? corporeal form?

a screaming cuts across the piano
a cop in a suit cuts across the screen
they both have more unearned confidence
than whatever spirits i can summon on good days

i don't like my mind and it's too literal a phrase
but i'm searching for susan sontag on the bookstore shelves
and isn't that enough of a metaphor?
forget the illness or the potential or—

all i want is salt on my tongue and sweet
and to not think about subtle increased signals
cold enters my veins from the left side
creeping fists clenched / who are they fighting?

my fingers form with the grip / am i losing?
white shadows on black
let me be your best american something
maybe then the lines will be clear

somewhere outside dogs are
barking / somewhere inside my phone
is humming / somewhere lying within
the machine asking / if this is a test, did I achieve my potential?

after all, i always was a diligent student

                    nobody tells me the answers to these questions

—DEREK YEN (he/him)

THE LIGHTHOUSE KEEPER TENDS TO MY CHRONIC PAIN

You arrive in song, light a lantern
within my body. Hot fingers singeing
the senses, twisting fascia until
I am a tight tremor of uncertainty.

Illustrious shadow magnified
in the glass, veil of the half self,
what do you seek in the long grass
of my existence?

Cut to concentrate, your beam
eclipses me with little effort.
Distance cannot compare
to your rotational design,

prick of light unfailing
in these depths. The air stings
and sea life cradles me.
Yours is a brightness that hurts.

Dysesthesia a hundred sharp pieces
wielded generously.
The hand that pierces darkness
also the hand to locate

the wreck stirring
on the ocean floor,
a glimmer of passage held
fast in its wake.

—SHELBY NEWSOM (she/her)

THE PAST IS AN INJURED THING

In my bad dreams,
I often see

myself still and voiceless
like a stone.

Your breath was warm
against my back,

but I cannot recall
where your hands were

or what you said. I had
a crystal—as white

as an albino mouse—inside
my pocket, and I held

it tightly summoning
magic. Nothing happened.

—RAQUEL DIONÍSIO ABRANTES (she/her)

there won't be a single shaman left

the world is still on fire but it's hotter now, more menacing
like i gotta watch my back every second though we've never lived
in a time with more peace. i'd like to believe that

but i'm deer-in-the-headlights-ing my way
through days, the bitter exhale of the end
rolling across the nape of my neck

my feet rooting like a tree trying to touch water
in drought, deep so paralysis is the way i exist
every moment is digging myself out of the grave

with a teaspoon. i must snap out of it. Cher is sadly unavailable
to help, and it seems like all the good gurus are taken.

how to pop open a bottle of lambrusco and have a nice time
is the name of my bestie's memoir but i can't seem to wrap
my mouth around the language she wrote it in. i see it all

crumbling in slow motion, too fast for my liking
for this time, there won't be a single shaman left
to hold it up. they're too busy looking out for themselves.

i know the strength to reclaim the narrative
is nestled in the palms of these hands.

i just need to blink before the car hits.

—MIRO (she/her)

An Attempt at a Poem that Contains Nothing But Truths

I like to be touching you. I read a lot
of books. I have five siblings. I like listening
to the same song on repeat. I have always
gone by the same name. I have loved you
for almost nine years. In forty-three days
I am going to take your name. I can pick
a favorite band, but not a favorite parent.
At most, everything I say is only ever
half-true. I'm excited to cut my hair off.
I can't wait to be married. I put stickers
on everything. My eyes are blue. I will not
write a poem for my wedding vows. I will
not have two last names. I have never
lain down in front of a moving vehicle
that didn't have a friend in the driver's seat.
I have never knowingly tried to lie to
myself. When I was ten I swore I would
never drink alcohol. I haven't eaten meat
in four years. I will love you for the
rest of my life. You promised I could die
first. And I will.

—Skyler Witherspoon (they/them)

SLIPPERY

I realise in the aftermath
you've got a fuckboy reputation
which is funny to me cos I really
thought you were a real lover
but did I bite too hard when you reeled me in?

I wasn't dominant enough for you
I should've had you on your knees but I lay
flat on my back for you
first time we kissed I should've said
down, boy! & had the leash ready
but I fucked up the dynamic by being too easy

What a shame
that you didn't stick around long enough
to see what I became
are you scared, babe?
of when I see you on the San Fran balcony
& smile? a little sad,
a little sadistically?

Cos if there's one thing you know it's
how a pussy feels
I know you wanted leaving me to be as
easy as having me but
you made up a narrative in your head
about it not being romantic
you weren't writing a monologue babe
it was a two character dynamic

I was there,
I heard what you said I saw how you looked at me
is there insecurity under that confidence babe
you shared everything but that with me
did we get a bit too deep babe?

was I the best fish in the sea?
is fucking with love too slippery?
were you afraid to hold on?

—DEVON WEBB (she/her)

Let's put everything we don't need in here.
I'll toss in my boundaries while you toss in
your criticisms and snap judgements.
I'll throw in my grievances with work
and you throw in all the baby names we
won't ever get to use.

We could have easily done this at the
kitchen table or in our neighborhood café,
but the hole opened up within distance of
our workplaces, so it made sense to come here.
We were silent the whole drive over,
the only voices being from your
Gotye-themed Pandora station.

The dumping ground was already starting
to fill, so soon after opening.
If I gazed into its abyss, I could see
admissions of guilt, unspoken declarations,
and a few bags of garbage from those who
confused it with the landfill further down the road.

We could add to its depths, roll a piece of paper
into a cone to really shout our words into its maw,
but that would require me to share the idea with you,
and neither of us have been in the mood
to be chatty with one another lately.

I figure we'll finish dumping it all in
and drive home to watch *Abbott Elementary*
reruns before we go to bed.
I'll add visits to the ground to our
weekly schedule in place of Date Night,
since this seems to be the only time
we're really committed to each other's company.

—ALEX CARRIGAN (he/him)
Title comes from a riff from the Mystery Science Theater 3000 episode Tormented

UNLOCK ME

> *—In response to Valerie Maynard's painting,'Get Me Another Heart*
> *This One's Been Broken Many Times'*

Keys
so many keys
     writhe inside my bones
jangle in rivers
        of discord

     force their way
        through my flesh
     search

         for what I can no longer see
        no longer feel

 I clutch
     at my heart
        my quim

but still

     I break

—CHRISTINE FOWLER (she/her)

THE QUEEN'S CARP AND A MAN WHO NEVER MOVES

a bowl—too small for dreaming:
carp shuffle beneath her porcelain smile.
breadcrumbs, sculpted like decrees,
drift—sharp enough to gut

→ the man sits in unlit air,
skin peeling varnish-thin.
light barges in
full of itself.

he is a tree that forgot how to grow:
wooden hands folded over
silence louder than breath.

courtier's velvet shoes tap rhythms
into dirt. no one listens.
his gaze could fell forests,
but pigeons steal her apologies.

behind codpiece—sea churns poison;
pocket—a hawk's talon crumbles to dust.

"spring," she breathes,
pouring water over spines
curving questions no one asked.

the carp bubble polite rebellions
too small for history.

the man imagines chaos:
glass shattered,
breadcrumbs scattered.

but they won't leap—and neither will he.

fragments of a haiku slip
through fingers stiff as bars.
"better to let it go,"

he mumbles to emptiness.

dust dances in unwelcome light.
the queen leans out—kissing pigeons,
the courtier broods, carp circle.
and the man remains.

light keeps coming in—
uninvited.

—SABYASACHI ROY (he/him)

FLOOD SEASON

My heart holds all of my firsts.
The first breath of life,
the first cry cracking out of my lungs.
It holds the rupture of a dam my parents tripwired,
so the flood has always won.
The guttural scream of you and sixteen,
a ruthless rise in your grip for the ripest fruit.
I was only trying to hold on.
To hold on to innocence like the *sun* prying
at time on the horizon just to catch a
glimpse of the *moon*.
My heart holds all of my firsts,
the shushed cries and soiled flesh
I did not pray for.
God crying in December's fog
as you abandon me in winter's thaw.
You are *forgetful*,
but my heart *remembers* all.

—MAY GARNER (she/her)

THE WAITERS

The giant ship moves slowly out of port
cautiously into the lagoon as if
it doesn't want to be noticed
between the ice creams and Americanos.
It's the only thing we look at, of course.
And if we remembered how the old town
was constructed—and when and by whom—it
secedes into the sticky rounds of jargon
and all the colourful boats in our foreground
pass us by.

The pastries still flake. The fillings are sweet.
It's the way we'd really like to recall
the best of our friends from the best of our years.
And is that rain in the air? When it hits
the vast expanse of water it's as if
everything stops and it's what we waited for.
What will we do now the moment is here?
Are we aware that something is happening?
As soon as it starts we'll move on.

The waiters, rushing to clear the tables
are practiced in all this grizzly psychology
feeding us the crumbs of returning home
where we'll curve our attention to other matters.
Sail on, they wave, as we leave.
When we get there we still won't know.

—MW BEWICK (he/him)

Hungover Again in Columbus, Ohio

11:30 a.m.
Saturday morning enough.
Hungover again,
I walk my United Dairy Farmers coffee up
High Street,
dragging my unclean face
astride my unwashed thoughts.
Bitter me, I try to leave myself behind
on every bitten-off corner. But
like the hungry ghost of a dog,
myself follows close behind me.
As I round 12th,
a blessed tree shades the concrete.
A house finch perches on a blooming branch
and sings.
Its red breast challenges mine
to a contest of warmth,
and today is the worst day for it.
Tomorrow I'll be kind again or even
this afternoon, if the others are lucky.
How thick a shadow I've built up
over the years.
Over my headache, I insist
the sun has done nothing to earn
its brightness.
Me?
All I have is bought and paid for—
and don't I look the part?
Stupid, singing, beautiful bird,
little demon,
loud villain,
why did you have to mend my day?
I was having a perfectly bad day, and
you ruined it.
Don't you know me by now?

How little I wish to be sated?
How bloodlessly I beckon, how soon
I'd start again?

—TY ZHANG (he/him)

DIAGNOSIS IN THREE ACTS

ACT ONE: As a trash bag

Rotting hotly on the sidewalk lie the treasures of her life
She sits—limp
misused
perturbed
Decades' worth of steaming vomit spilling from her torn-up belly

Once, she was new.

A modern marvel—tidy beacon even for the messiest rooms
Hailed by her inventors—men with questionable intentions
"She is the answer!" and everyone exhaled.

Glossy-eyed they ran to offer her their darkest treasures,
        their dust bunnies, dead cockroaches, moldy mandarin peels balled-
            up candy wrappers bloody needles dusty hairballs tear-stained
                ripped-up letters to long-lost lovers whose love hurt more
                    than the scars it left them with

In she took them
mouth wide open
body stretching to fit it all in

Her seams popping,
        rotten egg falls out
Her bottom leaking,
        trail of old blood

They drag her outside
And lock the door.

ACT TWO: As an anchor at the bottom of the sea

Some try to drag her all the way to shore
        They may die along the way
        Or succeed

Others gaze endlessly at the dark ecosystems in her every crevice and fall
to pieces at her grotesque beauty and use her as the deepest mirror
anyone has ever seen, ever finding their reflection farther and farther from
a light source they can barely see so they close their eyes and start to sleep
inside her iron body and build their nests out of dark water and self-
abandon and wait for the next one to plunge down here and think what to
make of a life heavier even than the sea

ACT THREE: As a wildflower in a field on the side of a mountain

Sunrise nuzzles up the mountainside and
cousins sisters mothers lovers stir,
each one blooming to the other

Toasty, sunshine-covered eyes unfurl
        Feel those stems,
        girls, how's it going?

Filaments reach for breath
        Aaah, still got it
Someone yonder won't recover

        Focus now, here's the bird!

Buzz buzz needle prick
        Hold your dirts!
        Damn beaks getting rougher

Petals dusted, ovules jostled
          Straighten up dolls and
Pray for the others

Perfumed slow dance to the breeze
Squalling through a faithful huddle
Bundle into dusk and pray for another

                              —CAROLINA MURRIEL (she/they)

TANGLED GIFT

Bubby Florance and I share
a tingle-tangle of necklaces.
She has many.
I have only one
a gift for turning five.
Our necklaces
          hang from our necks
when we chop-chop eggs, onions, potatoes
for Kugel
Our necklaces
          glitter golden in the sun
when we hang sheets and pillow cases
out to dry
Best of all Zayde has taught me
That my *aleph-bet-gimmel* necklace
Is like a bud which opens into a full blown flower
Inside lies a girl
afraid she'll forget   something important/to untangle her curls /to ask
for MaryJane's/not to use curse words/to tell her tears to water her
dreams
          But all the words of the world
                    are on her tongue

—LYNNE DOLLE (she/her)
Jewish myth, The Necklace of Letters, (Jer 6:19)

BIRDING

The grandma who caught me a stray green parakeet with her bare hands
was the same grandma who, with those same hands
taught me embroidery on a piece of pale green cloth

almost the color of the Swinhoe's white-eye
who flew into my other grandma's apartment the night of a typhoon
turning her slipper into a momentary safe harbor

The only kind of bird that grandma liked
was the kind on mahjong tiles
so Twit Twit found her home and name

with the grandma who let her fly
free in the apartment
returning to the bamboo cage at night only to rest and sleep

I will not but I am afraid I will
forget the twittery whispers my grandma made
as she pitter pattered around her home

speaking to Twit Twit in a tongue
that closed the distance
between woman and bird

the sound I now mimic
to close
the distance of time

—SHUI-YIN SHARON YAM (she/they)

Observing "Urban Francis" at the Weatherspoon

In thirteenth-century Italy, St. Francis
gave up his wealth for a life of poverty
and spent the rest of his days
preaching the Lord's Good Word.
He believed that hardship
brought him closer to God.

On a rainy day in the late 90s,
Judith Shea witnessed a man
in New York City staring up in awe
—at nothing.
Kept that image in her head for years
until she decided to sculpt it into bronze.

He's here with you now, still
looking up, wanting:
a dark figure, cold and yearning
in an oversized coat that swallows
the man-shape beneath it whole—
eyes forever enraptured. Feet bare.

His only friend, a placard asking,
*Is he transfixed by something actual,
or spiritual?*

Try to meet your eyes to his,
hover into the blank space—
is it the lumpy bronze
that grips you?—the imperfect marks
of fingerprints smoothed over?—

Or are you still standing here
waiting to hear a cry—
of pleasure, of pain—of something
so innately woven
into what it means to be human
that we're all still screaming it—

even silently, even now—even
the man in New York back then, staring—
and Judith on the train, in her studio,
sculpting—St. Francis,
on Italian cobblestone, suffering:
something we've all been craving—
like rainwater to our thirsty bellies.

—HAILIE COCHRAN (she/her)

FOG

Feels too   static   a word.
     My brain   rides sinusoidal   waves of supermoonbeams
     over the Sea of Tranquility   toward the Tributary of
Silence.   Takes a left past   the Depression of Time.
Notes   I
                                        need
to search   for where I've heard the line
about   moonbeams before. My brain swarms

stained-glass windows   with missing panels.   Tips
     my tongue to   .   Tingles of gentlefire
inflammation licking   up my skull   my scalp. Throws
function into furnace heat   powering a steamship engine. Drifts

through water   with purpose   then runs out
     of steam. The smoke
     the steam the water filled with porpoises   roiling
boiling

maybe fog isn't the worst   word. Conjures mystery
swirls the color of cream on   cinnamon. Gray matters
     oftheheart.   Axons tangled
     the way wires always end up noted.   Knotted.

Substantiating contradictions   afflictions include substitutions.
Throw away   the laundry. I mean I put it away.
          Fabric pressed. A vision   a blur
          unclear thick air   drunk into lung. Thin-necked

          bottle of breath   pinched
behind the eyes   knotted knowledge swimming
past steamships through streams   of blood. Streams of soup
          straining broth   through a sieve

        collecting   intentions   for today
anotherday.   The forecast reveals
a different soup   of the day

                                        for tomorrow.

                                        —DEREK YEN (he/him)

BLIZZARDS

Bitter winter touched my skin.
I fed on spear-wort and hungry minnows.
I found you, hounding.
I caught you in a net.
My hands thawed.
Mama spurned grass spears.
The hills froze with lances.
I sang into their veins.

—CONNOR FISHER (he/him)

DEAD LAND BEAUTIES II

The riverbed becomes the canyon
in that
you've never touched the bottom
in that
you haven't felt what might be
soft or graveled or
sharp enough to puncture what's
calloused
in that you can't lift
up and know
the sky overhead for the
glaring wild
that opens and opens
above you like a wooden
box caught in the
grip of
perpetual motion.

The blue
heron tosses calls
through
rippling-glass echoes without
snapping its beak. What
tears across
your chest cavity
flecking shards of gold
thimbles
and dry ice
you can't name or even
feel unless you
name it but you know
it
silent as an owl slicing
through the
dark.

Behind the chain-link
fence another moment muted

in that your
knuckle
slicks back your brow
and you rub the grey flesh under
your eyes and you
refuse to put
your
finger on anything.

Before a body becomes dust again
it claws
out
of deep-bellowed
desire to
grant salvation from
e n t i r e
abandonment. From the
incontrovertible truth of coercion
to nothingness.

But you don't know the doctrines
of mortality. You
know which
corner of the parking lot cracks
open at dusk. You know
which
candles clock-hollow
against each other. Whose
eyelids
burn fire-bright burgundy and slide
into black-line
horizons and whose snap shut
when they close. All the

blood and salt of
coveting. You know

the hand
as a heartlocked syringe and a clovering
root hideaway and a bittering agent and a shock force
vacuuming
out
your breath.

The dry scorch becomes the scar
in that
longing never mattered.
In that
the ghost of youth blitzed ionizing has come to scrape
the film from your corneas
so they shine again
now from catching wild glare
and to coax
from
your constricting organs the question
that never
ascended into your throat. You

walk beyond the dandelioned edges
of this ball field and tell
yourself: when you reach the foot of this
river you will stop
knowing only

what
you've known.
The riddle that has left
so many pieces of you empty

but kept you
whole.

—STEPHANIE JONES (she/her)

Mirror the Soul

In the night,
Harsh candlelight flickering against pale skin
Again & again
I trace the visible wounds
That shadow me.

How I prayed for these scars,
Under the thrum of cold showers,
Pinched skin, &
Sore ribs
With abandon,

Yet I
wallow in the thorns, a phantasm
Of corded muscle
& the near-flight
Of a full-body.

But to
Chase smoke and mirrors, shirk the day
& tie stones to dirty shoelaces
Only sinks the soul
& falsifies the prophet.

—Kai Grenham (he/him)

THE DOVES FELL OUT OF THE SKY

I think of you when I see yellow roses bundled at the store for young lovers.
They remind me of a day in late June,
an overpriced gown on sand,
my hair so tight I can barely move my face to smile.
They smell like the champagne that I drank solely out of tradition,
for you know that I loathe the taste.
I ate a petal once
to see if it would taste like lemon cake
with vanilla frosting that is not so sweet I could barely consume a whole slice.
It was much worse,
almost like drugstore lipstick
that I have never worn once in my life—
except perhaps as a rebellious preteen.
I suspect drowning them would not take away the yellow
no bright white would appear,
a new beginning.
In a fit of rage, I played dress up in my old gown and heels,
took the preserved bouquet,
and crushed it with the sharp points still speckled by the sea.
I screamed until I laughed
which turned into anything I have ever felt flowing from my eyes.
I fell to the ground, next to our flowers
feeling what it must be like to be them.
If I demolish everything that dominated my very being
for such a long era of my life,
forcing them to feel the ache that lives in me,
maybe it will loosen the death grip on my heart.

—KATELYN STUMP (she/her)

My Clothes, Their Wrappers

The first time I found a mound on my stomach, I told myself that I'm still a healthy girl.
When I got wider hips, I told myself that it'll make child rearing and bearing easier.
Kept telling myself that as long as I can see my feet, it hasn't gone too far.

Making deals with the deposits,
When my arm fat could rival an animated old man stuck in an emperor's banner.
Where I would have to push around my stomach to shave in certain positions.
To be gaslit by doctors from the PIN code to my body that they pin me down for.

When my legs hit any position against a seat,
I'm ready for mountain range guilt in multiplication.
My fat, the original colonizer.
From neck flub to swollen ankles in thrombosis.
Taking only face pics with your head tilted as upward as you can go.

Because after my mom got lifesaving gastric surgery,
She would brag to everyone how little she could eat.
And modeled wearing the same size as a child as being the only way to go.
Because my little sister is about to make the same deals.

My neck and arms droop like the tears when I could only eat crackers to save my liver.
My hips pour out with stretch marks in tow.
As the salt from the drenched crackers leads me one step closer to one less pound.
If only it worked that way.

I terrify of how my skin will age with me or how much rounder my face can become.
How many opportunities I will miss due to discrimination.
I would know how easy it is, since I was the first person who ever wrote me off.

Yes, little sister, welcome to the club.
Avoid all dressing room mirrors and clothing stores.
Don't let those designed funhouses trick you into the girdle mom threw on me.
Please never let your deposits anchor you to a lower confidence.
Or stretch marks tear you away from the truth.

We come from a family of people with bigger bodies in a culture of Slim Jims.
The tabloids already scream out how late I am.
They shout "Google Earth" and it's my picture.
My thoughts are the ones who took it and framed it in the first place.

—TAYLOR KOVACH (they/them)

I'M MOSTLY OKAY, WHICH IS MOSTLY THE TRUTH
—After Courtney LeBlanc

I'm going on vacation knowing I still
have a mouse running around my apartment.
I did try to catch it before I went, called
maintenance to lay sticky traps, checked them
before bed and when I woke up, even
put some peanut butter on one trap the day before
I left, but the little fucker observed me and knew how
to tread around the traps, how to climb into my trashcan,
and probably figured out how to excavate the
hole behind my oven that maintenance filled in
last time a mouse invaded my home.
Perhaps I could have tried harder, bought
more lethal traps or staked out in front of
my oven and my washer with a shotgun
for when it came out. But that would mean
accepting the role of a killer. That I would
harm something weaker than myself. Or it means
I really am too lazy to have my own home.
Too poor at maintaining my space, at regularly sweeping,
at choosing the right apartment complex to live in.
I'm going on vacation to forget all about
mice, traps, and poor apartment management,
but instead I'm just thinking about how even I
can't escape from the idea that I'm no better
at navigating this life than a common mouse.

—ALEX CARRIGAN (he/him)

THE TRIUMVIRATE MADE WORK OF THE WEAK

   1.

Here and there
People can pick up a guitar,
Give it a strum, a ripple in its heart,
Make a neat,   lush sound.
Then, they can put it down.   Walk away from it.
For a while, even. No need for any art—they even say,
We have no time to play, Guitar.

   2.

The inside of a guitar is empty,
And the inside of a guitar looks like a little house,
With casket walls, thick bracing,
Barren of furniture, of people.
A guitar is like my house,
I'd say. My house is extra empty when I leave—
I wonder if it misses me.

   3.

But it's just a guitar.
Not a gun, with fuses and pistons,
It has no shells but its travel casing.
Not even an atom to split.
It is empty, made to be plucked and stringed,
Played and tuned,
Prim and pretty,
You.

—MEL MANCHENO (they/them)

WHEN WE WENT UP IN SMOKE
(*for ancient outliers*)

Where were the monuments?
Misused wood, soot-covered roots
one tooth, a shred of homespun cloth.

Orange embers rose like fireflies.
We left memory, recorded only
by the air:
wing movements of stunned crows
warned the forest
of our fire.

—JULIETTA BEKKER (she/they)

WHEN MY NIGHTMARE WAS A HOME

When I lived in
the basement
of the shepherd's house,
I followed a line
of ants to my bed
every night. I start
the story here
so you're not
fooled by the bookshelves,
the comfort, the strawberries
and the fig tree in the garden.
The shepherd talked
to herself, and I lived
amongst her art.
I lived buried under
all the things she kept hidden,
everything she hadn't yet
finished. I surfaced for
food, for water, for her
to teach me how to leave.
And what could have
made me go for good
but the certainty I was
no longer safe?
When I lived in the basement
of the shepherd's house,
I would go days without
seeing another soul.
I filled the silence with
voices without bodies,
and I never felt half
as lonely as they foretold.

Once I came home
to the shepherd's basement
to find thousands of
tiny corpses piled in

every room. When
you've been gone
from a place long enough,
it turns either paradise
or hellscape, with no
purgatory left to
tell the truth. Everyone
wants a simple story.
But there's nothing I
ache for like the place
that haunts my nightmares;
nowhere I'm more
glad I left, and nowhere
I'd rather return to.

I have not seen the shepherd
in years. Yesterday, I
saw an ant in my kitchen.
I killed it, and spent the day
lining the room in cinnamon.
I say a prayer to a
god I've forgotten,
and promise that I will
stop pretending. Tomorrow,
I will invite the shepherd
to my wedding. If I'm brave,
I might even thank her.
But tonight, I will go
to bed, following
nothing on my way.

—SKYLER WITHERSPOON (they/them)

LITTLE RED RIDING HOOD

Wolves do not eat people often
and they never concoct elaborate plots.
But the huntsman will kill them.
He will even cut their bellies open
and fill them with stones and laugh
at the horrible grinding death.

"That wolf would have eaten grandmother
and an innocent girl," he'll say,
years later, when he points to his cloak
made of wolfskin,
no longer stained with blood.

His conscience doesn't howl.
He has fed it with stories.
It curls at his feet,
red and grateful.

—NOAH BERLATSKY (he/him)

a glitch, a lag, an apology

and she says *origin* like an apology—
        composite / not complete—
a wrist, not the hand
        // a vowel   mid-bite
                held in the teeth like a coin

I answer in syllables
        unaligned
a tongue shingled in mistranslations
        [mother] becomes *mudra* becomes metal

"where are you from" = glitch
        = lag
        = buffering history through the cracked screen

in the garden
        curry leaves snap in the cold
                (call it
        inheritance)

someone whispers my name wrong
and I nod
        as if that version lives here, too

—SOMRWITA GUHA (she/her)

day one: dysmenorrhea

do you ever just
scroll until your phone dies
but that is not enough so you stay
up all night learning
a new skill that cotton thread will
look pretty but it won't keep
that monstrous thing within
the refrigerator repair
man is here cutting
short my feverish dream
please help me sir
my life in the ice machine
pickle chips for breakfast where
once was your kiss
three 90-minute meetings gnawing
Ls one four five two and three
glory to spiders and their exoskeletons
would that my bones could keep me
in
fuck it
you have to take a shower
nasty everything
seeping
from swollen *follicules*
dna drowning down the drain
how many liters of blood
crush a hot tidal wave
against the firmament
of my skin
whisper warm licks across
the chaos outside
my pubic bone
traverse the fibers
of my underpants
do you ever realize
it's 3 PM now

unfortunately i have missed
the golden light
again i have missed
something i don't know how to find
between my legs are the jaws
of a hungry dragon
hunting down the reason
you had to leave
rooting through the icebox
cold again
i stuff the ghost
of an apple in my mandible
three melted cookies no more
your gifts
levitating in pursuit of
tangled jasmine to scrub
the stench of your left armpit from my right shoulder
i need something stronger
than blocking i need
an exorcism
burning in the rays of hell
at the shore of the bayou
purify my skin of the rancid
sweat of your midsection
pulsing
from my lower back the visions tell me
you will live until the day
you take your last breath
or until the day
you bury your lover
and if you are lucky
you will
bury your lover
and if you are even luckier
your lover will
bury you
between my legs

is the mouth
of a sated jaguar
snaring
you
in

                                      —Carolina Murriel (she/they)

SCARIFICATION

The night you died,
the sky wept with me,
running its fingers down my spine
with lightning scars to
match how I felt beneath my skin;
you were always afraid of the storms,
clinging onto me with claws and teeth
as if I had any other choice but to stay—
the thunder kept me there,
pounding in my mind with the rhythm
of your heartbeats, slow and sudden;
now the lightning does it for you,
raking talons like knives across my skin
to mark me yours.

—ALEXIS BARTON (she/her)

LET US LET US PRAY

Let us let us pray. Let us.

Let the circle circuit the maypole.
Let the angel of six wings find rest.

Now is the hour.
Now, the gap. The space in the ellipsis.
The space black out to the edge
of the flowing, reaching bang,
shrapnel of creation.

Let us now see what demands to be seen.

Blessed the word. Let us speak.
Blessed the sentence. Let us serve our time.
Blessed is the now to let us listen.

Let Francis calm the wolf.
Let the birds write their own canticle.
Let the son strip off his mother and father
to join the poor poor and laugh at wealth.

Now the dance.

Let Joan listen and burn
after gaining the boy his kingdom,
who gave herself to the stake because what else?
She listened, still,
as she ashed in the marketplace for the spectating crowd.
Then, scattered on the Seine.

Now the journey.

Let the two thieves die
with legs broken and lungs choked
and protocols followed, bit players, like each of us.
The torn Temple veil.

Let the skin be touched electric.
Let the door open and slowly close,
sorrow in the moment after, flight of another lost soul.
Fertile, multiplied. Spasm rhythm.

Riding the bubble, kicking the flesh-wall embrace,
pilgrimage to light.

Now and at the hour—

Let us let us pray.

—PATRICK T. REARDON (he/him)

The Tender Garden

My ego haunts the building.
My hound sulks in the rat's nest.
I harry you.
My sister shakes her hands.
Mama packs my trunk.
Mama lingers on a hymn.
My sister plants a tender garden.
Mama starts over, oiling your tongue.
Mama eyes cigars.
She spits.

—CONNOR FISHER (he/him)

the onion sits on the counter

for so long it sprouts, green
shoots in tubular sprigs,
growing in twists out of its head
& i have been out of my head,
i mean my mind, for weeks
with the move coming up & so
much to pack or throw away
on top of my general out-of-mind
post-viral brain & the internet
tells me these onions are usually
softer & more bitter to taste
& my doctor tells me i am sleep
-deprived, but i can't bring myself
to throw it into the trash, the onion
i mean, not the brain or the sleep,
it feels like waste, like killing
something alive & i rarely think
of my fruit as alive, but the oranges
& avocados & persimmons all live
& age on the counter & we have
been living & aging in this railroaded
apartment for years & there are men
in washington who talk about waste,
but the baby rubber plant sits
in the corner alive even though it lost
a few leaves this winter & the pine
tree in the other corner, the one with
the window, is yellow & dead & i
failed to keep it alive this winter,
which sounds like something a politician
might say, "failure to keep alive," which
almost is the same as killing & i think
the last time i killed something that was not
a roach was last summer when mice
ricocheted round the cabinets by
the washing machine with such speed

they approached quantum limits of here
& not here, they were schrodinger's mice,
probabilistic rodents & i caught one
on a trap, i felt soft bones with a thud
& the men from washington meet
with men from not here to agree
they are alive & talk about
waste & from here it sounds like human
waste, they said human animals & i
became the cat in this apartment, one
after another in my claws & i just
want the animals, the bees & owls &
whales to survive extinction, but i am still
out of my head, i threw the bodies of mice
into the trash & i am afraid the men
in washington want to see us dead &
red & yellow onion skins curl on
the counter like tapestries or people,
full of stories & tears sit in the corners
of my eyes without even picking up
a knife to cut the allium's layers
& how could they call it waste
& this onion has been cut before
even arriving, broken from roots, from
soil, no water but the wet in air & still
here green arms rise to find what little
sun peeks through the window in
the corner & the books next
to the tree already stacked
& ready to go into boxes
& if it keeps a person alive,
then how can it be a waste?

—DEREK YEN (he/him)

FOURTH OF JULY

I teach her the heaviest word: mother.
It anchors the page, wipes stray sand
from the corners of her mouth,
admonishes:
"We don't eat the beach." She's silent
except for a mind so loud
it rivals fireworks.

—JULIETTA BEKKER (she/they)

The Silence That Raised Me

I was born beneath a whisper never fully spoken,
a cry that never made it out of the cradle.
My name was stitched shut, down my own throat,
before I ever learned the sound of it.
There is a version of me,
still hiding in the basement,
below the concrete,
stuffed full of silence like insulation,
mouthing my misery through the floorboards.
When they bid me hush,
they didn't know they were killing me,
chiseling a suicidal cathedral from my chest.
They didn't know my ribs were ivory pews
from a shattered altar, my throat a mosaic
confession, cracking to bare light.
Can you hear me now?
The hum of the daughter who survived,
in the crackle of my mother's pills dissolving.
The voice I set aflame, just to feel its warmth,
grows *louder, louder, louder* in sweet spring's defeat.
I fear to be the silence that raised me,
always yearning to be the sound that
burns the house down instead.

—MAY GARNER (she/her)

MEDITATION ON A DRESS ON THE FLOOR

This land is only mounded consequences—
let's add ours to the pile.
The future will come shortly.
It need only travel again the distance
between the front door
and the dress on the floor,
multiplied but one too many times.
Is this love?
Or the same old fear of death again?
When the poison and antidote share the same effect:
bitter medicine, all that I drink.
Time has begun to let slip
that there is no cure to this
most terminal disease:
I'll go years without feeling at all,
then in one night's span, feel so strongly
it's as if God himself were bleeding out in my bedroom.
But feel what exactly?
There's the real crime.
I fancy myself a plain dealer, so precise.
So precise, yet there's not a single thing I've felt
that I can name.

—TY ZHANG (he/him)

THE DERPS AND THE DS (A RAD PISO)
—after José Lezama Lima

cyclical   vinegary   slap   slap   we talk
        cravings   urine   the sardine   the diamond   sex cascades

a horse to water   im on the floor   looking at comets   severely merry   in fleshy symphony
        when i meet yu   deliquescing in blossoms of salmon light   what a YAWN

        i make fun of yu   yu feel USED   from waist to taint   my day polished
        by the whites of white lotus   the backwards explosion   it's unjust

        in yr throes of vaginal withdrawl   my secrets hurled   dripping w dew
        ribs exposed   yu find relief in cupid's slips   abusing my benevolence

        yr vengeance is a topaz drenched in tobacco   but i'm still a dolphin's tortoise
        my nose is a slide trombone   but yr still terrified of birthmarks'n'bottled water

        OKAY SO LIKE   wrapped up   in security'n'mysterious   flattery
        daz ultra-chaos   crushed   from head to toe   it forebodes

our impenetrable touch   DONTCHAKNOW   there's a drought   i met yu
when dawn didn't disguise us   i carried yr day   but clearly   yu haven't learned a thing

—EMILIANO GOMEZ (he/him)

Q&A I

Do you save your loved ones' voicemails?

I'm not sure how many sisters I have. When
we're together it's always a party. I used to
have friends, and now I see them in a coffee
shop. I hear my name come out of their mouth
and never see their eyes. I can listen to them
say my name any time I want.

What's that big box in the attic?

Everything was worse quality then. I don't
have most of the originals, only copies
saved and crammed together. Once
he wrote my name on a piece of paper,
and I can prove it. Once this flower meant
something to me. I don't remember why.
The ghost of love is all I need to keep it alive.

Why are you worried they'll all disappear?

This is the fourth car I've seen him drive.
My first kiss was sitting on top of one. If I'd
still been there when it flipped, I'd be halfway
through the concrete. Ostrich head buried in the
sand. Once a girl said she liked my dress.
Once a boy played a bloody game with me.
They're both dead now.

Who are you kidding?

I'm good at keeping things. Worse at
labeling them. My brother told me to tell
people when they're right, just so I'll remember.
I told him no. It's more fun this way.
Sometimes it's better to guess. Sometimes
it's better not to know the answer.

—SKYLER WITHERSPOON (they/them)

The Vulture

That we might walk quiet through the woods together,
afterwards bare-chested in the sunlit clearing,
our feet mud-slick from the soft earth's pull,
burrs clinging like old stories to our ankles—
that was all I wanted. No phone. No noise.
Just the moss, the hush, the sound
of your breath beside mine.
Sometimes sweet tea in a flask. Sometimes silence.
But lately, I've stopped praising this world
out loud.
How the forest opens
not suddenly, but with ceremony
the crooked path bending toward my childhood,
the smell of bark and sweat and my mother's hair oil
simmering in memory.
The trees breathe heavier here.
They lean in, say things in bark and birdsong,
ask questions I don't know how to answer.
And I, barefoot and dizzy from the mushroom's
sacrament, am just now learning how to listen.
Isn't that how it is?
You wake one morning, lit from within,
your blood humming gospel,
then hear a child's body washed up in a river,
somewhere far but familiar.
And no amount of crying can undo
the weight of what we've done to each other.
What kind of man am I?
What kind of son?
I think of my uncle,
who put the liquor down one day
and never said why.
Just sat quiet in a busted lawn chair
under the pecan tree,
a book in his lap he rarely turned.
The light would fall on him like grace.
Sometimes he'd nod like he knew
a secret he couldn't share.

When he took me to school,
we said it'd be a good day if we saw the vulture
circling the big pine at the edge of the freeway.
If we didn't, I'd feel a little less protected.
Then he started to lie—
say he saw it when he hadn't,
or that it flew off just before we passed.
And I'd lie back.
Say I'd seen the wide wingspan too.
That it was there, always there,
even when the sky was empty
and the pine had been cut down.
That's the real truth
the things we say to carry the day.
The vulture was there
because it had to be.
Just now, I felt I should be alone awhile,
in the clearing with my grief and the trembling ground.
But then I looked up
and the trees were reaching for each other,
and it felt like they were praying,
or maybe I was.
And I saw you
the way your shoulders bent forward in thought,
like you were building something delicate
from the bones of your past.
And even if I fail at everything,
even if the world keeps spinning mad,
I want to point to the vulture, like I was taught,
want to say: there—look
the black wing blessing the sky,
the thing we see
when we stare long enough

—RAIS TULUKA (he/him)

Breathing Black in Appalachia, New York

Fear lifts no ridges here,
so I bend, furrow shadow into melody:
a hymn rising from buried roots—
a vow of springs stitched tight to the Allegheny's soil.

Keeper of air, I:
full-lunged, unyielding,
the tang of bark and cold creek water
pressed deep into my chest.
I do not shrink.

Wane not, but weave:
Delve;
draw
inward toward the ember.
A quiet once foreign,
now familiar,
woven deep into this earth
where echoes hum eternal.

These valleys know hands,
know songs carved in stone,
know the weight of timber pulled from hills.
They remember me.
Not by name,
but by the press of my breath
turning trails into prayers.

Black hands cleared these forests,
hewed beams and split rock into shelter,
left fingerprints on the grain of maple and oak.
We do not fade,
though silence wraps us tight—
we exhale,
wide as ridges,
loud as the wind threading through leaves.

Here, the roots are braided
with sweat and salt,
carrying the hum of ancestors
who planted songs
when nothing else would grow.
Their voices rise,
their breath lingers,
their shadows stretch alongside mine.

Breathing is rebellion.
Breathing is praise.
Breathing is the inheritance
of those who stayed,
who sang,
who sowed springs that never died.

—RICARDO NAZARIO Y COLÓN, ED.D. (he/him)

BATHROOM HASH

Consume the substance as it consumes the hidden
Figure she'd surely understand
Insanity at red eye. Why one drinks monsters like a marine.

Her children.
Roman candle father. Shrivels out before you can say
You piece of—

I'm here. Astringent orange blossom. Problem with authority.
Temperature stiff as a dead goose, Towels tossed in urea.

Miming the eternal wicker.

—BRYCE MAUZY (he/him)

PHASES OF TREATMENT

I rate my pain on a scale of one to ten,
undress, and lie face down on the table.

My acupuncturist starts by inserting a needle
in the crown of my head, works her way down to my toes.
Each needle strikes the soundboard of my body,

waking connections between tissues and cells.
She burns mugwort leaves—enveloping the small room
with its earthy, camphoric curl—applies heat
to my skin, stimulating the points that ache.

Brightness prickles as she places electrodes.
Have a good rest, she says, like always, turning off
the light. I lie there suspended
between a place of ease and discomfort.
When she returns, she asks for more time.

Cheerfully, my acupuncturist tells me
her glass cup collection has increased
since her sister's visit from Korea,
where they are less expensive. It is a relief
to have the needles removed.

To know the suctioned force that awaits
is far more predictable than earlier spasms.
Red and purple circles emerge across the span of my back.
For the next week, I watch them wax and wane,

a visual reminder of the throes of gravity
my body finds itself in.
At night, my husband traces the lunar outlines,

eyes searching telescopically for the source
of my chronic pain, both of us watchful of its orbit.

—SHELBY NEWSOM (she/her)

FOLDING IT UP, LETTING IT GO

Folded into a paper airplane, I toss you
    from the treehouse. You swerve
                through swings and glide over the trampoline
        where I taught you how to front-flip,
returning like a persistent horsefly.

Extra creases—you are ready
        to be pitched like a scuffed softball,
            out the other side, through the gap
                with a plastic pirate telescope
                we stargazed from, denying
                bits of dust on the cheap lens.

            Defying gravity, you soar
    up the slide, back to me. I crinkle
you into a crane instead. You taught me how,
with a napkin from a backyard picnic,
shaded by the treehouse shadow,
on the last day of summer
when the sun shined on us.
No drawn-on eyes for this new crane—
You cannot look back at me. I drop you
        into mud drying below, murky surface
            fractured by twisty birch roots.
                Splotches of muck soak your wings,

                and your paper fibers come undone.

—TAYLOR NECKO (she/her)

Abecedarian for My Herpes Girlies

ass out again i'm a sultry jazz
baby girl popstar in this monday
class where leather limbs
dance like sex don't you know
everybody who's anybody has hsv
for real! my dance teacher's one-eyed shih tzu
growls in the costume closet
hallways of girls line up just to pet his ears
i can't make this shit up i pop valacyclovir
joyfully each night my high kick iq
kicks higher *take it from the top*
ladies miss claudia claps two
manicured hands arthritic and sparkly green
never again will i claim to be lonely i'm
only fierce only feathers at the studio all
pretty angels are trans all pretty people are kink
quickly please mr. dj
rock us another beat kiss me or don't i
stopped caring a long time ago about how to arch
the best parts of myself i say look lovebug
ugly isn't real even if
viruses are
why stop this whole living thing when you could
x-step in heels and make sexy hip-hop magic?
you don't have to know everything just grab
zillions of glitter guns and drench the place you diva

—SOPHIE PEDERSEN (she/her)

between suitcases

i was told
we left   nothing
        behind

but i keep
finding   the wrong ghosts—

     saree folds   that remember
             my mother's back,
     the stiff tuck of a pleat
     like a closed question.

                tupperware that says
"imported"—
                plastic soft as memory
          but warped
          from flame.

my son eats with a fork.
he says:
        "your food smells like
                stories."

i don't tell him
        that smell is the last
        language
i still dream in.

                (meanwhile: a train station in 1999
                that never stops echoing
                in my knees)

                we live in rooms
          white with forgetting.

the rice still clings
to my fingers
     a warning.

my mouth,
        a torn customs form.

            where are you from
(pause)   which year?

—Somrwita Guha (she/her)

A SNAIL SHELL with monster truck tires. Tank treads on a lion seal. They rev their engines at the finish line, race backwards to the beginning, where the clubfooted mayor in a two-piece bikini waits to present the trophy cup to the victor. I watch the action from the living room window, grandmother balanced on my knee. For every blind turn the competitors navigate without crashing, she grows a little younger, until she is nothing but a black and white photograph of a baby. She lies naked on a bear skin rug, the spitting image of her mother, who was either a porpoise or a sea otter, according to family tradition. In the sky, drifting in from the distance: a giant cow's udder descends upon the city.

—JUSTIN HOLLIS (he/him)

DILEMMA

I don't want to write about
the way my mother braided my hair
as she twisted my tongue
into the vowels & consonants
of white people

But that was a form of love
the way a good spanking
is a form of love when it stops
the child from running
into the barrel of a service pistol

I don't want to write about
how borders
thick & penetrating
render my body a slab of meat
on a cutting board

No letters behind my name
nor green card or red passport
could shield me
from the blue line
that turns aliens into bare life

But when the CBP agent
from his high chair
admonished & flirted with me
in the same breath
I chanted:

"I could write about this"
conjuring the only spell
that could affix the most docile
coy, harmless, little
smile on my face

I don't want to write about
how my home became

the city of tears
where young people carry
their last will

Would the police accept
"Grandma, I worry
that you would cry
for me, but I cannot not go on the street"
as a valid form of ID

But they only listen
when I show them loose teeth
on the pavement and
smeared blood
stains on subway trains

I don't want to write about
the white woman walking
two Japanese chins, insisting
that I must have
some Japanese in me too

or the repairman in my apartment
who gloated with a wink
that I could be his
daughter from his military stint
which is to say, rendezvous, in Japan

But they always ask:
Tell us stories that cut
so that we can approximate
what it is like to be
a woman/ an Asian woman

an immigrant Asian woman/
an immigrant Asian woman fleeing
from one authoritarian regime

to another
show us all the marks

on your body
so that we can
self-flagellate and feel
how good & empathetic
we are

I want to write about
the way my dog's ears flop
as he runs down the hill
with a wild exuberance
that I will forever try to emulate

I want to write about
the contour of my lover's jaws
the notch between his clavicles
how his face fits
in the cup of my palms

I want to write about
my friends' teary eyes
as we gazed at each other
after watching Lord of the Rings on November 5
promising to hold each other tight

I want to write about
the suspension of time
when I play tag with my child
the whisker on her left cheek
as she scrunches up her nose and laughs

I want to write about
joy, in all its promiscuous forms

—SHUI-YIN SHARON YAM (she/they)

GOOD LOVE
            —*after bell hooks*

It's religious. We don't call it prayer
but we open like a book.
You raise a cup to my lips and we belong
to each other's joy. Jubilant, we hold,
we kiss the hands of spring. *Amen.*
Reluctant, we watch the memorial of a
dream.

Service is a kitchen table. It's friendly nods
on the bus. It's a park bench snack
with strangers in the winter sun. It's a slow
bloom of hope across a landscape of souls.

—JULIETTA BEKKER (she/they)

You do not have to do what you do not want to do. It's not supposed to be so casual that's a myth they told you. Or maybe it can be for some people & sometimes for you but so often another boy who doesn't love you right is no conquest just a burden. Just another memory like remember what they did to me. Remember what I did to me.

You don't have to call yourself low-maintenance like you're proud of it. You're autistic, even the simple shit's hard & sometimes the feelings come out like vape cloud confusion & they don't like it so heady & sweet. You deserve to be swept off your feet. To be listened to. To run out of things to regret.

You are not as submissive as you think. All this breaking makes you bold. Have you ever had a boy look up at you with that smile like you're miles & miles of miracles accumulated over time. Like you could go on & on forever or until your thighs start cramping. & even then your body feels like something perfect instead of hurting.

It doesn't have to hurt. Or it can in the ways you want it to but not in the ways that you don't want it to. Your body is no animal your body is you. Your heart is no extravagance your heart is true. You bleed red & your veins glow blue. Do not try to know a man who doesn't want to know you. He will not hold on.

—DEVON WEBB (she/her)

SWAY.

The chemical soup of my brain
changes color in the dark.

Feed me strange things,
nourish my emptiness.

The back of your chest
at the front of my mind.
Every day we talk
and never run out of voice.

Swinging and swaying while the food burns.
Caught in the warmth of this wondrous passion.

Invigorated,
like a slow running river.
Low-grade currents,
bubbling under.

Palms melt and mold into one.
Hear my heart through my spine.
Uncurl and unbend
the crookedness of my frame.
Count and mark the vertebrae.

You talk with your hands
and dancing eyes,
weaving a loom
of all your favorite words
in a song for me,
one too fast,
like the hummingbird's heart.

Break the hourglass.
I have decided
time no longer exists.

We are vast and varied,
formless, endless,
zero, even.
A quiet peace.

You, who seduced the moon,
hold immensity in your keep.

—Augustina Naanret Dasat (she/her)

FICTION

They only went out at all because Seth refused to do his business indoors. If Johannes had his way, they'd never leave the shelter of the house they'd grown up in, the house their mother left to them fifty years before.

Weird to think that for thirty of those years, Seth had been in his dog-form. If he'd been a true dog, through and through, he'd have died more than a decade before.

And now they were both getting old. Johannes understood that more starkly whenever the sunlight hit Seth's canine body askance and revealed a shriveled, naked man on all fours.

That was the trouble with their condition. There was always a risk they'd be in the woods, stroll past some youngsters, and sunlight would filter through to expose Seth.

The result would be screaming only suffocation could quiet.

It had happened just twice in three decades, but Johannes was extra careful these days, using his naturally taciturn disposition and a warning to stay back, as though Seth might bite, to keep folks from insisting on ruffling his silky ears.

The woman was a worry though. She smiled at Johannes and Seth each time their paths crossed, her uninvited amiability utterly bewildering.

The week before last, she'd approached as Seth squatted. Johannes flicked the shit off the path with a stick before waving her onwards, half hoping to disgust her into keeping her distance in future, and half trying to make the woodland track clean for her.

He didn't like that latter feeling. It reminded him of their mother and how he'd scrubbed the house each day to please her, long after she choked to death on a piece of pork crackling left over from the Sunday roast.

"I hope you're both well," the woman, the stranger, said blithely as she passed. Seth's huge furry head jerked at her words, and Johannes snorted his surprise.

She looked at Johannes with a bright twinkle in her eye that made him uneasy. Her skin and hair had an odd luminescence he supposed was down to good health, yet reminded him of a book of fairytales he'd found once in the kitchen amongst recipes. Their mother feigned bemusement when he showed her and then left it out on the lawn to mildew until small, frill-capped mushrooms sprouted through the pages.

Sometimes Johannes and Seth saw the woman, the stranger, on the track ahead, paused with her head raised and tilted as she listened to a green woodpecker's yaffling or a blackbird's show-off recital mashing mimicry with soaring sopranos.

As separate as they held themselves, as grumpy as Johannes kept his expression, she never failed to smile at them and comment on the beauty of the day.

It was irksome how she celebrated the ordinary. Nothing could prise the smile from her berry-red lips, not even the wind dragging the hat from her head and sending her hair into wild knots. "State of me!" she declared, chuckling with hands turned upwards as though in acquiescence.

Johannes baulked at the itch that stirred in him at the delight in her voice.

He was relieved to catch sight of another side of her one day as they walked uphill and saw her trip on an exposed root. She swore as she wobbled and regained her balance, arms flailing. Her voice dropped from its chiming cadence to something deep and rough.

Seth barked then, a sharp sound that seemed to catch her by surprise so she toppled.

"Oh, help me up then?" She raised a hand plaintively, and Johannes had no choice but to go to her and grasp her hand. Her skin was soft and he had a sudden imagining it might be fragrant, because women liked scented lotions and things, didn't they? Their mother often used something that stank of putrefying roses. And Seth, who had a far greater sense of smell in his dog form, was sniffling and slobbering at the woman, the stranger, so Johannes had to aim a sly kick to remind him to be cautious. Any shift of cloud could set a sunbeam free and expose him for the haggard haunch of a man he truly was.

"Thanks," she said, seeming unaware of the urges the two of them battled. She looked down at her knees, lifting one gingerly. "Oh, look at that. Another pair of leggings ruined."

Blood gleamed through the torn lilac fabric, painting her naked flesh.

Johannes swallowed. "You're hurt."

"Ah, it's nothing." She made as though to limp away, and Johannes ought to have let her, but she looked paler even than usual and his breath caught in his throat.

"We're just, we're just, our house is down the way here," Johannes gabbled, his pulse pounding in his ears. Seth glared at him with something that probably wouldn't look like anything to anyone else but Johannes saw warnings roiling like storm clouds in his yellow eyes.

"Come and get cleaned up at least," he muttered finally.

The woman, the stranger, smiled at him and said, simply: "Thank you. You're kind."

The closest entrance was through the garden gate and up the weed-straggled path to the kitchen. As he led the way, Johannes let the woman take his arm and lean on him, the weight of her unexpectedly warm. He grew aware of the staleness of his clothes and himself, and that the kitchen would smell much worse. At best, there were bowls and plates of rotting food, at worst, a dead rat or two dispatched by Seth.

When they reached the bench near the kitchen door, he halted. "Wait here."

He hurried inside, leaving Seth sitting beside the woman, watching her with every sense alert. He could hear the woman talking all the while he was searching for a cleanish tea towel and disinfectant, and boiling water in the lime-scaled kettle. What could she be saying to his brother? He glanced out and saw to his horror her winding her fingers through the fur on top of his scalp, and stroking his ears. Seth seemed frozen, perhaps shocked, as he had been, by her vibrant heat, or, more, likely, fighting the instinct to bite.

He poured steaming water into a salad bowl he'd wiped dust from, and dashed out. "Here."

She smiled, perched on the bench where their mother used to sit, her expression wide open.

Seth glowered, growling softly.

"Silly sod," Johannes said to his brother. "Make yourself useful and go and do the washing up."

The woman snorted. "Now, wouldn't that be nice?"

He handed her the disinfectant and she looked at it doubtfully.

"Do you want me to do it?" he asked, half irritated even as anticipation rattled through him.

"If you wouldn't mind," she said apologetically. "I'm a terrible baby about this kind of thing." The blood on her flesh shone as viscous as their mother's blackcurrant jam.

Seth growled once more. In that instant, clouds parted overhead and a ray of sun struck down, illuminating and exposing the man he was, in parts.

His body was not only old now, but thin and ravaged, with scant hairs trembling on his sinewed thighs and shins. His penis alone stood strong and proud.

"Ah, there he is," the woman murmured, even as Johannes flung the tea towel in a vain attempt to cover Seth's modesty.

The sun seeped over the woman like honey dripping from a hive and showed her pale skin to be transparent and writhing with veins as thick as worms. Johannes gazed at the stranger with her mouth wet and laughing; her gums drawn back deep into her maw.

And now he was afraid.

—JUDY DARLEY (she/her)

1. BANANA BREAD

Every day we asked ourselves if we should leave, and every day the answer was yes, only we didn't know how. We weren't old, but we no longer felt young. We didn't have it in us to walk away from the only life we'd ever known. We looked at all the others who stayed, who kept going to work and coming home and eating dinner and tucking their kids into bed like none of this was happening, and we thought, maybe we're the crazy ones. Maybe this is all fine. It didn't feel fine. But we had already survived so much history. We couldn't remember a time when we weren't afraid.

So we bought a gun. We hunkered down and made banana bread. We ordered a telescope online and learned the names of the stars. We brewed our own kombucha and built a chicken coop in the backyard. We drank too much and cried too much and sometimes slept in separate beds, or not at all. We told the kids, stay close to home, there are monsters in the woods.

And life went on.

2. THE WORM AND THE WORLD

There were four of us in the little yellow house in the trees on the other side of the stream. Me and Paul and Maddy and Cy. Cy was the baby, the one I worried about most. By all rights, it should have been Maddy— but she was nine years old, and I knew already that she was like me. Smart and strong and prickly, a born survivor. Cy was only four. I worried about him because he was still so soft and kind. I didn't want to see what the world would make of his goodness. I didn't want to watch it get crushed, or twisted into something self-serving and ugly. The color of his skin, the pale worm between his legs, the beauty already written so plainly on his face—all this meant he would grow into a world bound to give him whatever he wanted. Where he could lay claim to whatever he chose. I wanted to keep him small and sweet and with me, always. To hold him apart from the world and its awful possibilities.

3a. INSIDE WATER

The sound of heavy rain is widely considered to be relaxing, and this is probably true for most people. But it might not be true for you, if for many years you lived in an old house with an old, battered metal roof that was prone to leaking. In that case, instead of being lulled to sleep by the sound of rain lashing your roof, you might lie awake consumed by a terrible tension, trying to discern if what you're hearing is inside water or outside water. Inside water and outside water have different (though closely related) sounds, and you would know this if you had lived in an old house with an old metal roof that you never had the money to fix. Your body and mind would be alert to the difference. Even if you had since moved to a different, much nicer house (say a little yellow house in the trees on the other side of a stream), even if you knew perfectly well that your new roof was made of composite shingles in good condition, you would be unable to stop yourself from anticipating and guarding against the possibility of inside water, just as you anticipated and guarded against all the other catastrophes that did or did not occur during that time.

Just as you cannot stop yourself from anticipating and guarding against all the catastrophes that may or may not occur in the future.

3b. INTERLUDE/SCHISM

One night in bed, Paul says to me, Maybe we should give them a chance. Maybe what they're saying isn't so crazy after all. I scoff and wait for a punchline that isn't coming. Don't you ever get tired of losing, he asks. I turn to stare at the rise and fall of his broad, hulking back. He is either asleep or pretending to be.

4.　MECHANISMS OF STRESS TOLERANCE

Last month it was axolotls. But now Maddy says everyone in her class is obsessed with axolotls, so she has moved on. Her new thing is tardigrades. She reads me part of an article she found online. *The tun state challenges the popular idea that there is a hard line between life and death. A tardigrade in tun is not doing any of the things we associate with being alive, but it is not dead either.*[1] Sounds familiar, I say. She gives me a funny look, a cluster of tiny creases troubling her smooth brow. Like looking in a mirror—only my wrinkles don't go away when I stop frowning. Not anymore.

Maddy asks what fluorescing means. I tell her it's when something is all lit up from the inside, like the lightning bugs that have started to appear in the backyard. Earlier than I can ever remember, this year. But the world is changing. We all know it, we just can't agree on what it means. Of course I wonder about what she will inherit. Will she be able to go outside and breathe the air, have a job, walk the streets unchaperoned. Will there be enough water to drink.

I try not to think about these things. Everyone believes they're living in the end times. But so far no one has made it to the end.

5. THE LAST WALL

The house is getting smaller every day. Paul says I'm wrong, but I know I'm not. Every argument turns into this argument. He thinks I'm crazy, but he's too kind to say so. As for me, I think he's being willfully obtuse. There used to be more rooms, I insist—don't you remember? Our lives were once bigger, of this I am sure. But he'll see, one day. Soon enough, it will be impossible to ignore. I imagine the look on his face, the day the last wall disappears. And then what? Into the woods, I suppose. Maybe it'll be a good thing. Maybe a new beginning is exactly what we need. Beginnings are so beautiful, after all.

Paul will be a good provider. He's always loved camping, all that Eagle Scout shit. Of course, it's a little different when you don't have a choice. But we'll manage. We'll have eggs from the chickens, and the chickens themselves, if necessary, though that will be hard. Cy has gotten so attached to them. We'll spare them as long as we can. There will be fish in the stream, and critters in the woods—deer, elk, mountain lions. Our new life will be bloody and brutal, no question. It'll take some getting used to. But kids are so adaptable. Before long, they'll see that it's easy enough to kill something when your survival depends on it. More honest, too.

Soon we won't remember what it was like to live inside a house with walls to enclose us, or a roof to keep us dry and shut out the stars. We'll

---

[1] https://www.theguardian.com/science/2021/mar/20/tardigrades-natures-great-survivors

forget the days of staring at screens that told us the world was on fire. Our clothes will grow soiled and tattered, until finally we discard them. Then we'll roam the woods naked, exposed and unashamed. Our disordered proteins will rearrange and harden in novel forms to protect us. We'll live for a long time that way, in a world all our own.

Until one day we find ourselves fluorescing, our sad old human skin unable to contain us. We'll say goodbye to our bodies and to each other, but we won't be sad, because we'll know we're saying goodbye to hunger and weakness and pain. Only when the last wall has fallen can we be truly born again—as creatures of terrifying beauty, made entirely of light.

But until that day comes, I'll try to love the life I have. I'll look for the helpers and drink my thin milk. I'll do the laundry and make dinner and find new ways to keep the kids entertained. I'll try not to complain, I'll make myself small. Because each day brings me a little closer to the life I know is waiting for me. Out there in the woods, where no one can see.

—SARAH BRADLEY (she/her)
First published in Phoebe, Vol. 53.1

Wednesday, 4:15 pm

Hi, I was really nervous to send this to you. I couldn't get my thoughts together enough to speak, so I thought I'd send it as a text.

4:16 pm

You are the best thing that has ever happened to me. I'm so grateful that you're in my life. You're an amazing and beautiful woman. I never ever stop thinking about you. I want to be with you forever. Can I come see you today?

4:23 pm

Diamond, I love you. I am in love with you.

I tossed my phone onto my bed in frustration. My heart felt like it'd been tied to a brick and dropped into the Roanoke River. I stared at the black screen, trying to convince myself it was a prank. Or maybe a drunk text. But it was four PM on a Wednesday, and I knew better.

Panic set in at the thought that I would have to deal with this somehow. And fast. I picked up my phone and unlocked it. Read the messages over and over again, slowly. Scanning each word, hoping they'd rearrange into something less terrifying, somehow.

"I want to be with you forever." "I am in love with you."

Oh brother. My eyes picked up on the worst part.

"I want to come see you today."

Dread overtook me completely, fast and inescapable, like tear gas in a closed room. There's no quietly slipping away from this. He knew where I lived, my school, my job, and the coffee shop I frequented on Tuesday and Thursday evenings.

I sank to the floor, the carpet's greige fibers pricking against my knees. Elbows propped up on the edge of the bed. Phone clenched in both palms. As I searched for words to say, the typing bubble appeared.

4:34 pm

Can I come by later?

Sweat gathered at my hairline, and my palms went slick.

4:36 pm

You okay?

***

Three years ago, we met during freshman welcome week. Swapped phone numbers and started texting constantly, coordinating when we'd show up at all the freshman events. We stuck by each other's side, even as we mingled with other freshmen. From day one, we were together so much that everyone assumed we'd been childhood friends.

Freshman welcome week is chaotic yet crucial. It's where friendships start, even if most fizzle out just as quickly as they form. Everyone's on the same playing field, scrabbling for connections in unfamiliar territory and bonding over the smallest similarities.

Oh, you like Hello Kitty? So do I! Friends.

I have those shoes too. I'll wear them tomorrow. Friends. And, the most classic of all, having the same major. Friends.

We were in the statistics department, though he minored in finance. He seemed light-years ahead of me, already building the rest of his life meticulously like it was due at 11:59. He mapped out his entire future on a Notion dashboard: four summer internships, an MBA, a quant position at Citadel, and then somehow, venture capital. He was a self-help book purist. And he secured Internship #1 halfway through his first semester.

I was pretty clueless, and he took a liking to that. He took me under his wing, despite us being the same age. He found it refreshing that I was essentially a blank slate, with no parental pressures and no five-year plan.

The first semester, our class schedules lined up almost perfectly. The perfect excuse to hang out, constantly. We sat next to each other in the back of the class. Walked to the cafeteria together daily. Worked on assignments together. Most nights, we alternated between my dorm room and his across campus. And he'd always walk me back to mine at night. He insisted on it, for safety.

He became my closest friend. My best one. And, for a while, it felt like he made me better. I became more disciplined and focused. We'd go for walks, then jogs. Eventually, my family knew him by name. The brilliant, driven friend who was "good for me."

He leaned into that. Loved the compliments I gave him: accomplished, talented, smart. And he returned them with his own.

Pretty. Gorgeous. Beautiful. Pretty. Pretty. Pretty.

I set him up with a girl I met at an environmental action club. They went on two dates. Minutes after the second, he called, telling me she wasn't the one.

"What went wrong?" I asked, but he didn't respond.

***

Later that night, while sitting in my bed, leaning against my pillow, he looked at me and said, "She wasn't like you."

I laughed it off. Pretended I was thirsty again and stepped into the kitchen to breathe. There were so many moments like this.

By sophomore year, our classes no longer lined up, but he'd wait for me on a bench outside the lecture hall, saying he was "just in the area." He noticed things. When I changed my blush. Switched my lip gloss. He told me I looked "shockingly beautiful" while studying for midterms.

I could pretend I missed the red flags. But I noticed them. I hoped avoidance and playing dumb would cool whatever was starting to boil over.

***

Now, he'd sent a love confession, via text, on a Wednesday afternoon. I finally replied, trying to clear the air.

5:26 pm

I appreciate the compliments, but I don't see you that way. I've never seen us that way. I care about you as a friend. You've been my best friend, and I hope we can keep things respectful moving forward.

I read it over five or six times, trying to find a balance. Honest but not cruel. He read it five minutes later.

Read 5:31 pm.

No response.

***

I didn't hear from him again. So long to good morning texts and hours-long phone calls. No more hangouts.

A week passed. Then two.

Someone said they saw him at a party, dancing with a girl he'd met in his finance class. First came the soft-launch Instagram story. A mirror selfie, phone strategically covering her face. Then tagged photos. And just like that: a whole relationship, born out of thin air.

The next time I saw him was at the student center. His hand was around her waist. Sitting at the same table we used to claim as ours.

He didn't look over. So, neither did I.

137

But seeing them made my stomach clench. A sudden, sharp ache. It wasn't exactly jealousy. I didn't want to be with him. I never did.

But it was the feeling of something ending. Quietly and without warning.

Like a break-up with someone I never dated. An ex I never asked for.

—KIANNA AMAYA (she/her)

I always make eye contact with the flight attendant when I travel by plane, while they are doing their sacred dance. Everyone else with their headphones on and noses in their phones or eyes closed or looking listlessly out the window at the tarmac. It breaks my heart. The flight attendant looks like that kindergartener, in her tutu at the edge of the spotlight on the stage of the school auditorium, peering out desperately into the darkness of the crowd hoping her dad has arrived—her dad who has never ever showed up. So I watch intently, like that little girl's mother. With eyes trying to say, "it's ok, I love you, let me be enough, like how you are enough." And the attendants point their fingers and sweep them delicately across the aisle, step in unison, listen for their cues, make every quick change. It is so brave to do their dance for all of us, and important too, and what I am doing is also important, because I think it gives them strength to continue.

The flight from LAX back to San Francisco had been delayed several hours without reason. I had, by this time, been on the road for weeks. Mainly by car. This was the last leg and I was calculating, making bargains about how much junk food I could eat for every extra hour I had to wait, if I should open Sniffies and find someone to fuck me in the bathroom with my eyes drooping from sleeplessness, whether I would go to that party I had booked this flight on this day at this time specifically to make it in time for.

We almost boarded before they informed us a tire needed changing. And once we were on the plane, the bodiless voice of the captain said it would be a few minutes to file the paperwork. Thirty minutes later, after I had completed several games of solitaire on my phone, the captain began a long and methodical description of the modernization of airplane mechanic paperwork processes. It has been moved online now. There are three forms which must be filled out, verified, and signed. When each one is completed, it is updated in real time on his screen, so he knows they are making progress because one is already done. This used to all be physical. Pieces of paper delivered, checked, voices over the radio confirming airplane identification codes against documents and take off times. It is so streamlined now. We are 5 hours behind schedule. Over 7 commercial passenger airplanes have crashed in the US this year and it is only May.

I am traveling with my mandolin, which I play proficiently but not professionally. Sometimes I like to find a quiet spot in an airport during a long layover and play to myself. When I travel through Los Angeles, it feels gaudy and I keep it wrapped in my jacket, worried someone will accuse me of trying to be famous. When I board planes with my mandolin, I ask the flight attendant whose job is greeting you as you enter the plane if there is a safe place to stow it. I have watched people crush their hard shelled suitcases against my mandolin in the overhead luggage compartments. Once, after landing, I found two strings broken. Although later a friend told me this could be caused by the drastic elevation changes during flight affecting the tension. Either way, I feel better when it is tucked in the first class coat rack.

And if I'm being honest, it feels like a travel hack, or a special exception, and when I leave the airplane an attendant will remember me, and make sure I got it, and ask about what's inside, and I will feel a little dirty taste of fame. When I boarded the plane from LAX, I was so tired and the flight seemed mainly empty and anyways it was Los Angeles, so I kept my mandolin with me and put it, wrapped in my jacket, above my seat.

After all the digital paperwork had been virtually verified and submitted, we pulled away from the terminal. I kept nodding off and in the moments I was more conscious, I regretted not putting my mandolin in the coat rack in first class, pictured it tumbling at impossible angles and snapping its neck. The flight attendants lined up, carefully counting out their paces between each other to ensure they were neatly distributed and each had enough room for their big moves: oxygen mask drop, infant life jacket inflation, above-wing exit sweep. I took off my headphones and pinched my thigh hard to wake myself up.

Recently, I've been picturing myself being a mother. Everyone always tells me there is no rush, which hits as a cruel reminder that I cannot bear my own child, that I'll only be a "mother" in the legal sense, and that can happen whenever, within a reasonable distance from death, like writing a will or establishing a trust to reduce the tax burden on said legal heir when they receive said inheritance. I need to be as present as I can for their dance. If I can't be a good mother for 5 minutes to these flight attendants, then certainly I can't handle the pressure of being such an intentional mother as to coordinate the possession of a child completely non-coitally.

The flight attendant who is performing for me, a few rows ahead, has full lips and so much sorrow bunched up in the corners of them. I think about the US magazine I read at my cousins' house one summer in middle school, try to recall the details of the elusive "smize" or "smiling eyes" which I think would well communicate a sort of empathetic love without offending the sorrow in his lips. I can't tell if I am just squinting, or scrunching, or maybe blinking, and eventually resign to my signature slow, mild smile which I have perfected in many motel mirrors to show support in moments like this.

It can take a long time to catch a flight attendant's eyes. They are searching everywhere. They don't know yet which face is there to support and adore them. I wait a long time, almost until he does his final procession with the quick left right turns of the head. But then, before the origami moves with the safety pamphlet, we lock eyes. He pauses and the pamphlet slips out of his hands. I gasp and stand up out of my seat. I begin clapping to the beat. *Clap. Clap. Clap.* He picks up his pamphlet. When he stands back up, he is crying. I take my pamphlet from the seat back pocket and walk up the aisle toward him, stomping each step into the carpet to maintain the beat. I hold the pamphlet in front of me with straight arms, and he matches me. We unfold, I mirror with the left first, then the right. The left in, then the right. He only looks at me. I am his safety. He finishes with a flourish, the pamphlet tossed into his pile of props. I made it all the way to him and wrap him up in my arms. The lights in the cabin go blue and dim and we sit down in my row. He sits down in the seat left empty beside me and falls asleep with his head in my lap.

—JOSIE YACONELLI (she/her)

We were visited by the coyote again.

It was a particularly rainy afternoon in October, which I suppose is not uncommon for the Oregon coast. But the wind was heavy, blowing at sixty miles per hour. The weather channel was calling it a bomb cyclone. By the evening, we, along with everyone else in the area, lost power. All the light and heat had gone. Nayeli and I sat bundled up in our blankets in the darkness of the living room as a single candle flickered between us.

She explained to me that storms like these are common in México. The rain and thunder will come on like *that!* She clapped her hands together loudly and I jumped back in surprise. From the somber tone of her voice, I knew she missed the storms. The force of the thunder. The excitement as lightning flashes across the sky. And the large puddles left in the village streets after the downpour ends.

My sister and I would have to find things to preoccupy ourselves, Nayeli said. *We'd light a couple candles and read to each other or play cards. One time we even made a ouija board out of paper. You should have seen the look on our mother's face when she found us! She was so angry. She's a very superstitious woman. No surprise there. And I think that movie The Exorcist—you know the one where that girl's head twists all the way around—it had come out just the year before. I think that made her even more superstitious.*

As the hours went by and Nayeli's stories continued, the candle began to diminish, melting into itself and coughing up a final thread of smoke before going out. At some point, we too went out like the candle, drifting asleep where we sat on the floor. By the early morning, the power had returned. And so did the coyote.

First, I should tell you what I was taught by my parents and my grandparents and their grandparents before that. There is no such thing as death or afterlife for us. Well, perhaps not in the way you might imagine. We die, but then we return. When we pass on, my abuelita told me, our past self, shaped by everything we were ever made of in our lifetime—our memories, our wisdom, our pain, and our goodness—returns in the membranes and cells of our new body's flesh. We will be different but our body will remember everything.

This is how I know with all my bones that my little brother is the coyote, the sand-colored pup with a glowing white chest. The one with skinny legs who wobbles by our home each day with small objects in his mouth. He drops them in the same place by our garden, in a scrap pile that has grown to at least half a foot, maybe more, in the last few months. Today, he returned just like yesterday. This time with a beaded necklace dangling between his teeth.

When he was alive, my brother Elias collected many things: old beer bottles, often broken or chipped with sharp edges; pressed flowers and dried autumn leaves; sprigs of lavender, which filled his pockets with its balsamic aroma; yards of shed snake skin; and shells, mostly oysters and abalone fringed with a deep purple color and shimmering mother-of-pearl.

Elias and I would wander along the beach near our home in the mornings, when the tide was low and the ocean had drawn back far enough to reveal brine-scented sand, wilted seaweed, agates, crab husks, and on occasion, the washed-up bodies of dead seabirds, fish, and even large whales.

While visiting our family in Colima one summer, Elias treaded on the corpse of a pelican on the beach. He was only six at the time. I remember he returned home crying and cradling the poor creature in his arms. He told me he killed it and said he was sorry. But the pelican already smelled strongly of decomposition. And though I explained to him that the bird must've been dead before he found it, I believe he still blamed himself— like he could have prevented it from dying. Like death could be stopped in some way. Because of this, Elias became obsessed with saving things. Living things, like the tired and dehydrated bumble bees he'd find on the pavement during the months of extreme heat in summer.

He once nursed a stray kitten back to health. After a rainstorm, he found her hobbling with an injured paw on the street. He fed her and washed her flea-ridden fur. She never left his side after that, following him everywhere. So Elias named her Sombrita, his little shadow.

Elias began saving objects too. He'd stuff countless trinkets in his pockets until they became so full they'd tear and burst open. He kept oxidized jewelry, bottle caps, frosted sea glass, and bird feathers. He would argue these objects are also living things. *They have memories just like we do. That's what makes them worth saving.*

After Elias died, I found a page in his diary that read:

I smiled reading his endnote. Ever since reading about Pompeii, Elias became obsessed with geology, particularly earthquakes and volcanic eruptions. He'd learn a new fact and share it with me and Nayeli. I was so sure that one day he would be one of those scientists in his books. I imagined that he'd travel to remote places, discover a hidden underwater river or a lost continent, and return from his trip with his wide, gap-toothed smile. Then we'd sit at the kitchen table and he'd tell us every last detail, down to what he ate and wore each day.

The entry was dated the second of June. It was a Tuesday. A week later, just days before he died, our aunt Nayeli gave him a handmade wooden chest for his fifteenth birthday. I remember how his eyes lit up when she pulled the white sheet away and uncovered the chest. He stored all of his treasures in it, sorting them by color and shape, with the most fragile objects—wrapped in old rags, cheesecloth, and tissue paper—resting at the very top. And the final object, just beneath the lid, was his diary. He had strung a satin ribbon through the gutter of the final page, bookmarking where he wrote,

Last night I dreamed that I was a coyote. Tía Nayeli would probably tell me it is a bad omen. She says they are tricksters and thieves. But I felt so free! More like myself. Just like a scavenger who searches for and saves the most glorious things. Things that I bet others would just leave behind.

—ISABEL LEMUS KRISTENSEN (they/them/elle)

"When's Misha coming over?" the Anton asked—his younger sister, Maika, behind him—voicing the question on both their minds.

"Oh, he's not coming. He's in Russia. I forgot to tell you he texted me yesterday morning. He flew to St. Petersburg. Strange—so suddenly." The brother studied their mother's face as she relayed the unexpected news. For more than a decade, Misha—Mikhail—had been a sore subject. Whenever she spoke of him, their mother's face seemed to tense up with consternation and weight. Seeing that same expression now—when the news should have calmed her—puzzled them.

"Really? Oh—we just had some gifts prepared for him. Well, I guess we'll give them to him once he's back." Anton barely hid his surprise and silently wondered whether Misha would even return. Maika stayed silent, her face inscrutable. Moments earlier they'd compared gifts for him—Maika's father, her brother's step-father. Slippers, a mug, and an ill-advised embossed lighter. Misha, the constant presence on Novy God evenings, year over year, despite his divorce from their mother. Where else would he go? Back home to St. Petersburg, apparently.

"Mom, Adler will be here at, like, 8:00 pm."

"Good! Tell him to come hungry."

Adler. The little sister's (little no longer at nineteen-years-old) boyfriend. She had made a habit of calling him by his surname to differentiate from her brother's name, Anton. Whenever Anton was made aware of the boyfriend, he couldn't help but wonder about the awkwardness of their names being the same. He felt that in some way, he'd been inconveniencing her. But, being older, he'd worn the name longer, and that was that. He considered the upcoming dynamic, which would consist solely of his mother, the teenage couple, and himself: a newly separated 29-year-old. Anton suspected Misha's sudden absence would make the evening run more smoothly. It would be less familiar, yes, but smoother and not as awkward or tense. And though their mother's face seemed strained, he was sure her spirit would be up come the time of the festive dinner.

For the time being, Anton retreated to the room out of which he lived, where he hid as of late. He wore a synthetic Santa hat to invoke holiday spirit, and felt in a rush to read as much as he could before the year's end.

His eyes were held by arrays of sentences glowing softly out of an e-book's screen, his sole refuge. The room was cluttered with book-laden boxes, a large suitcase, and darkened computer monitors. The glow of the room was aureate-orange. The lamp out of which light emanated had long since lost its matching, bedside twin. Carson McCullers' words on the immaterial page pertinently—and painfully—spoke of *the immense complexity of love*. Of a loving husband. A suffering wife. And somewhere in the room lay hidden and shineless a forlorn ring of gold. For a breathless thirty-six seconds, it had once hugged a slender finger in preview. *Keep your eyes closed—don't peek!* In the impatient, curious act, a malign star eclipsed a benign one. In the lapses of attention to the words of the book, Anton's inner eye looked up at the preceding year's fireworks, the toast made then, the intimate presence by his side. The incredulity of how things had fallen since then. His eye wandered too far, too freely, and was yanked back with force to focus on the pages of the book. His door creaked open before he could begin the next short story.

"Anton, look!" His sister ushered their elderly dog into his room. Her long nails—long overdue for a trim—clacked on the floor tiles. The grey tones of her fur, since she had been a somnolent puppy, had compelled Anton to jokingly call her *starinkaya babushka*—old granny. The loving nickname had taken on a tinge of sadness in her advanced age. It was much too accurate. Her name was Alpha, as she was christened by his sister. Their mother had always told them that as far as she was concerned, Alpha would be her omega. No more dogs after her. Alpha's grey fur was dominated by the lush red of a small sweater, and a comically small Santa hat held on her head by unseen elastic. She waddled in, seemingly shy about her new outfit. The sight warmed him.

"Oh my god, it looks gorgeous on her. And the hat! Let's go, let's show mom." He got up from the bed with renewed energy.

"Mom! Check out how Maika dressed up Alpha." They gathered again in the kitchen, where their mother added finishing touches to a modest dinner for four. Her green eyes lit up at the endearing sight. Some days, the mother's love for pets—for animals—seemed zealous and driven by the heartbreak of eventual loss. Even in happiness it was always possible to see the beginning of grief, had she time enough to arrive at the all-encompassing conclusion, the tragedy of it. She could bear just one more.

A knock at the door took their attention away from Alpha. The knock was met with Alpha's retaliatory, anxious barks.

"It's Adler," May—Maika to her family—unlocked the door to let him in. Anton Adler had his reddish, curly hair cropped short and stood less than a head taller than her. He gave Maika an imperceptible kiss on the cheek, then turned to navigate the low-grade discomfort of greeting her reticent older brother, and her much more approachable mother. With Adler's arrival, the apartment's shape shifted from an intimate circle to a semi-circle, revolving around him. Maika took the lead and the guidance of him into the traditions of the holiday and began to recount how such nights typically progressed. To her brother, who stood by the dinner table to arrange plates and dishes, the flow of their conversation inevitably reminded him of a time when it was his turn, his holiday to share, his girlfriend to bring into the fold. Anton considered how their familial traditions had gradually gone through a process of dilution, and how invariably, detail by detail, intricacies and meanings were lost. The version of Novy God as retold by Maika was recognizable, though a far cry from a Novy God evening somewhere in the distant turn of the millennium.

"And there's this movie we always watch, it's super long. Mom, what's it called?" Maika trailed off with embarrassed laughter, as if unsure of why the retelling was necessary, but feeling compelled to do so nonetheless.

"С лёгким паром! Or Ирония судьбы. It means 'The Irony of Fate'." And the film was summarized with sedimented memory. A tale of mistaken identities and the falling in love of strangers, all set on a snowy Novy God eve in the 70s. Though the mother retold it with cheer, it could not pierce Adler's polite lack of understanding. Anton, quietly waiting to see if any help was needed in explaining their family's quaint traditions, thought with some envy and distaste of Adler's large, well-off family. Adler's eyes were observed for any signs of derision or mockery, even though he'd done nothing to earn the suspicion.

While his sister and mother were occupied with Adler's initiation, Anton took in the decorations they'd set up that morning. They were a coalition of festivity, decline and meager means. Thanks to Maika's initiative, the living room was run through with bands of neon lights and papercraft decorations, and the centerpiece—their aged, plastic *yolka*—sat laden with a mixture of vintage, Soviet glass baubles and a sundry assortment of anything that could hold a spark and a shine, anything playful. Through the synthetic yolka's needles and branches ran the black snaking of a wire punctuated by fairy lights rotating through red, green, and blue flickers. The faux tree's base was hidden beneath a bunched up, silken tablecloth, standing-in for snow. Soft lights, familiar magic—and yet . . . Anton suppressed a lump in his throat and turned to sit at the table, trying not to think of the yolka he'd forgotten to take back. *What did she do with it?* His unintentional inauguration of the dinner table made his mother formally invite everyone to take their seats. Mother beside son, sister beside her beloved; and the head of the table, where Misha would have likely sat, imposing, inconsiderate and in a world of his own, was occupied by the hungry, wool-clad Alpha.

"Well, Maika, let Adler have a taste of everything! Anton, have you ordered the sushi yet?" Their mother's voice was marked by the amusement of letting a novice try unfamiliar dishes. She didn't seem to mind sushi being part of the holiday dinner, either.

"Yeah, yeah. It's on the way." Anton quickly replied as he considered the ETA displayed in the delivery app. Anton did not expect the idea but agreed to it when Maika suggested it earlier that evening. He turned to look at how Adler fared with the traditional dishes.

"Oh, thank you. But . . . I don't know, it's kind of not my thing. I think I'll stick to the sushi once it's here." Adler shied away from the plates which held the variety of Novy God dishes; Olivier Salad, the purple mound that held salted herring within, the savory aspic called Holodetz, slices of bread adorned with the translucent orange of caviar, and the various platters of cheese and sliced sausage.

"Come on! You have to try at least a bite! I'm getting you a bit from everything." And, as Maika resolutely collected an assortment for Adler to reluctantly try, Anton felt proud of the surprising defense of the holiday, its dishes, and—by extension—their mother. It was the least they could do with generic sushi on the way to push the Russian dishes to the edges of the table.

Anton rose to pour red wine into a mismatched foursome of wine glasses, or were at least two still a perfect pair? He wasn't sure. The wine was bitter, dry, and in large supply, as it always was—their mother's favorite. She'd already been nursing some as she was preparing dinner.

"Ok, children, come on. I want to raise a glass to you." The siblings and the earnestly adopted Adler raised their glasses with attentive eyes leveled at the mother.

"Children, I want you to achieve everything. You're so smart. I believe in you. Really, truly do. The only thing I need to be happy is to see you succeed and love. So, to you. And may you always be healthy—the most important thing in life." With that, the four glasses softly clinked and jostled the wine cupped within.

Anton, with some discomfort, wondered whether his time in the limelight of their mother's wishes had ended, whether her wish was mostly directed at Maika and her promising boyfriend. He couldn't fault her if that's how it was. And as he tilted the glass until red bitterness rushed into him, he was suddenly keenly aware of how little they spoke in Russian. Of course, it was to accommodate Adler, who didn't know their language. It was natural. As natural as how rudimentary Maika's Russian had always been, and how their mother no longer bothered to use it when speaking to her. Russian seemed to slowly retreat from their home, as it did from the table. It was kept there no longer by Misha's unyielding insistence, or Anton's gentler attempts to separate the outside from their home. A rattling buzz from the door put Anton back on his feet. He pulled off his hat and went to the door.

"That must be the sushi."

The introduction of the sushi platter to the center of the table changed the tone of the dinner as all took morsels onto their plates. The only wine glasses to refill were the mother's and Anton's. Motherly questions and interrogations were then sounded across the table. A curiosity and vicariousness and the desire to know a life in bloom; daughter of her. Her sole confidant as of late.

Maika, as did Adler, tried to satisfy the mother's enthused curiosity, and in doing so, brought cheer and laughter to her face. Her face. Neither Maika nor Anton noticed how it had aged and changed shape, how it wrinkled, how it bloated, or how undeniably age 56 occupied her body. Whenever they caught a true glimpse of her face, as Anton did, sitting by her side, the reality of it pinched and sent fear through the heart. And though she laughed overjoyed at life, even offering sly remarks or jokes, which was known to Anton exclusively as the domain of either Misha or his own father, he could not shake the underlying truth of it: their mother was chokingly alone.

He eyed the dwindling liquid in their mother's wine glass and could see how sometimes it was a coffee mug or a glass meant for water. He could see how the glass was sometimes left in the morning at the foot of the couch. He could see the source of the liquid as well: empty bottles finished alone. Her flushed, blotched cheeks. The emotion pouring out of her as the red poured in. He could see grocery deliveries coming home, jingling with a force of more than two or three bottles, bought in bulk. *Maudlin mother, do you not drown?*

With everyone having had their fill of the selection of dishes, or just the sushi rolls, the table's wealth was switched out for a sweet variety. The creamy lushness of cakes, a few donuts brought by Adler, some chocolates and gleaming, ornate teacups by which to sip black and green tea. Anton consulted his phone for the time: 11:07 pm.

"Oh, the new year's already happened in Moscow."

"Wait—we missed the countdown! It's what my dad usually does. He makes us watch the live countdown from Moscow. He always counts that as the *real* new year." Maika offered the explanation to Adler, though did not venture further to speak of his absence that night. The topic brought a hush over their mother, who simply sipped tea out of a cup, as if waiting for the invocation of Misha to dissipate from the conversation. When it did, and with a wealth of minutes remaining until midnight, each enjoyed their own brand of sweetness, and slowly wandered about the living room as the TV hummed with canned sounds of celebration. Time passed imperceptibly.

"Mom, I think Alpha is scared," Maika broke the lull as she called from the couch, where she'd discovered Alpha lying balled up and shivering.

"Oh god, it's the trauma from the firecrackers," their mother offered with worry and protectiveness, "She knows it's coming. She always does."

"Aw, well, we won't do anything loud this year. Alphachka, it's ok. Don't worry," Anton moved over to the couch and gently smoothed the white, soft fur on her head, then pressed his palm against her side to feel her shiver in waves. It was then that his phone rang with an alarm. *Three minutes left. Hurry up.*

"Mom, where's the champagne? Freezer?"

"Yeah, should be. Is it? May, get the glasses from the table."

Everything sped up. Anton found and held the biting cold of the bottle as he tried to prime it. Maika handed everyone mismatching champagne glasses, then took Adler by the hand and made them stand by the tree. Their mother flipped the channel over to a local countdown.

"We always stand here with my dad, and we aim for the tree if we have party poppers," Maika's hands hurriedly gestured towards the glittering yolka, "So the confetti adds to the decorations!"

Anton's heart swelled at the unexpected pride in his sister's voice. The meager traditions even he let go of. And yet there, in Maika's voice, they were loved and unshakeable as they'd always seemed. She simply believed.

"20 seconds!" He held down the cork, already feeling the mounting pressure and gush of bubbles held within the dark glass. His hand slipped.

10 seconds.

"Mom, we forgot the sparklers!" Maika called urgently, squeezing Adler's hand.

"No time!"

Four, three, two, one—

С Новым годом! С Новым годом!

And so began another year of love. 2025.

—ALEXEI RAYMOND (he/him)

The classroom window was warped and wouldn't close all the way. When it was windy, it shuddered and the room grew drafty. Ms. Hanley stuck a wedge of folded cardboard against the frame. She had done this for the past four winters.

She turned and looked at the room.

Twenty-six desks.

Fifteen textbooks.

Twelve chairs with a wobble if a student leaned too far back.

She jotted the items down on a list she had been keeping. She thought someone might ask someday, but no one ever had.

That night was the annual school board meeting. She smoothed her hair, adjusted her skirt, and took a long look at herself in the mirror. Her heart thudded loudly in her chest. She had been in the district for more than ten years, but tonight, she felt like a stranger in a room full of sharp eyes.

She had paced the floor of her bedroom last night, willing herself to be ready. Tonight she would explain it to them—compel them to hear the need for the small things—a few simple supplies, one working computer, and some new copies of *To Kill a Mockingbird*, the ones the students still had to read with pages taped together.

It wasn't much. But it was . . .

She stood in front of the empty room, her notes in her right hand. The words she had rehearsed in her mind ran together, mixing with self-doubt. What if they didn't listen? What if they only saw her as a beggar with her hands outstretched, hoping for scraps? But no, she couldn't think like that. She wasn't asking for scraps.

She was asking for a future. *Their* future.

When the time came, she crossed a few hallways and entered the auditorium. It was half full, and most of the people already looked tired. The fluorescent lights hummed, flickering in the back. She caught a glimpse of the school board members sitting in their seats, their pens poised, their eyes glazed. The clock above the stage ticked steadily.

She could feel it, a wave of heat that crawled up her spine, making her cheeks flush, her hands tremble. The room felt too big. Too bright. She stood behind the podium, gripped her notes, and waited for her name to be called.

"Ms. Hanley," the principal said, his voice a monotone.

She stood up, her knees creaking slightly, and walked to the microphone. The air in her throat felt thick as she spoke, her words heavy, like they were coming from someone else.

"I want to thank the school for giving me the chance to speak," she said, swallowing.

She motioned to the notes in her hand, her eyes skimming the list of things she'd written down: the desks, the drafty window, the cracked linoleum floor. She mentioned the textbooks, the lack of resources, the students who stayed late to clean the chalkboard and sweep the floor because the janitor couldn't be spared.

She tried looking into the audience, but the eyes were too much for her. So, she kept her gaze fixed on the darkness just above the heads in the back of the room. And while she did, she pictured their faces while she said their names.

"Nathaniel," she said softly. "Grace, who has been helping organize the library. Samuel, who wrote me a short story last week."

She named every student and then sat down quickly, hoping the heat in her cheeks would settle.

The principal blinked at her, his expression unreadable, before offering a stiff smile. "Thank you, Ms. Hanley," he said. "You have some . . . passion."

She tried to breathe.

The meeting carried on: the gymnasium floor that needed replacing, the plans for the prom budget. She sat there, the words running together as she waited.

Her stomach churned.

It was late by the time she got home that night.

***

Ms. Hanley woke the next morning and drove to school, her mind still whirling. She unlocked the classroom and switched on the lights. They blinked on one by one, a few flickering before they settled into brightness.

She noticed immediately. Something was different. She stepped closer to her desk, slowly. There, in the middle, sat a shoebox wrapped in crinkled construction paper. A piece of masking tape on the top bore the words, "For the New Books."

Her breath caught. She blinked hard and opened the box. Inside were a few crumpled bills, some sticky pennies, and several folded notes. She unfolded one of them.

"Mom said I could use my allowance."

She swallowed hard. Another note: "Thanks for all the fun reading times."

She sat down slowly in her chair.

The students began to trickle in, taking their seats. The chairs creaked. The room was quieter than usual, but no one said anything. Everyone pretended not to notice her eyes.

A long moment passed. Then she stood and cleared her throat.

Outside, the cold wind rattled the window. But she didn't hear it this time.

—Zary Fekete (he/him)

"Then why'd you say it," he asked. Exasperated. Beyond sick and weary of breathing identical breaths over and over like a leaf when it touches down on the soft, autumnal loam.

It falls upon deaf ears. The blood drains, more than ruptured, it's annihilated.

"Have you ever been beyond the want of desire." The words he wished he'd voiced.

It's the hollow feeling he gets when her lies plunge like anvils into his skull. His skin is a thousand and one bee stings when she makes but a whisper through desiccated lips. It's the messes and lessons of which either propel or cease a life.

It's what he's learned in reliving it again and again. Like flotsam washing up on the shore, it was their lack of harmony that compounded the wreckage. He waded through it. A rusted nail caught his foot. He understood.

Nevertheless, he breached the threshold to the point of no return. It was the entire span of the demarcation he constructed. It collapsed, and she heard not a word he professed. It was as if he were keening to a ghost.

There is no other light who can provide him what he yearns. Consistently. Other than himself. And what he loves.

"It's not often I reach," he pled to her. "It's when I need you the most."

Twice in succession, and she left him adrift. He was a child in the lea. There were rutilant ambers and reds for as far as the eye could behold.

"You couldn't pull yourself away from you," he lamented. "The lie is your truth."

It was the epitome of their existence. She blamed him for what she could not control. He blamed her for not knowing the difference.

The strength in her defense was the fatal flaw of self. Of fear and reaction. Hers was as scant as gossamer. He peers through her every thought. Her whim is his bane.

"If I promise to be exactly the thing you swore to me you adored, by declaring the vows we transcribed the night you found me on the shore in the sand, then what, there is no what, only why." It was the last words to her he ever spoke.

Tears and rebellion and torn sinew followed. It was never enough.

And when he bled out on the bathroom floor, it was she who opened the vein . . .

The great wisdom he gleaned from death, is in death, he was finally freed to roam the halcyon blue in peace.

And that resiliency is not of the meek. With no meaning other than this: It's a release from burden. It's the truth of the blind.

To witness the ember as the spark. Then emerge unscathed from the sepulcher paved in the fallen of those before us who've drowned.

Hubris is the blade of conceit and man's interminable want. That the world can fit in the palm of a single hand.

Played out on a string as the skies fade from crimson to ash.

—DYLAN NIGHT (he/him)

1. The Bite

The wobbly ceiling fan above my bed moves so fast that the blades are a grey blur. When I was a kid, I was worried that it would unscrew itself from the roof and slice me up while I was sleeping. So, when I was awake, I would keep a very close eye on my fan. I would watch it swing around and around in violent circle after violent circle.

It clicks each time it completes a full loop, in perfect metronomic rhythm. Suddenly, I cannot focus on the fan, because you have loomed over me in a glacial canopy. My flesh becomes goose-pimpled and raised, as you lazily drag your icy limbs across it; the hairs on my arms, the fullness of my lower belly, the stubble on my legs, the peaks of my hips, all parts of me are lifted in resurrection.

Every ambient light in my room is switched on and buzzing. Glowing against their warmth, you are practically transparent. I can see right through you. It is as if you were made up entirely of honey-coloured light, some golden spectre descended upon me like an angel!

Not even a whisper could fit between us now. I want to melt against you, for your body to become my body, for your skin to become my skin, for your pulse to become my pulse. It is so easy to distract myself with your unearthly beauty as you crush the air out of my lungs and take in all my breath as your own.

I swear I can hear the lamps humming in perfect synchronicity. I am worried that they have been left on for too long. I want to reach over and turn them off, but you are open-mouthed and desperate. So, I let them murmur to each other. They speak low and sonorous. I can't make out what they are saying; I am scared they are talking about me.

You are charting a map of unfamiliar terrain. The lower you get, the more I can see the fan again, so I start to keep time. Inhale, as your lips hover over my chest; hold, as they plough through undiscovered curves and bends; exhale, as you raise your eyes to look at me, and flash a wide, toothy smile. Inhale, as you begin to move again, invading and conquering new flesh.

Teeth. I can feel the edge of your teeth at the junction of my neck and collarbone. My body goes still and quiet, and I cannot look at you.

Instead, I think of the time I got oral surgery. Stretched out in the long operating chair, making shapes out of the black flecks on the ceiling, as the orthodontist approached me with a needle. I have never been able to watch the needle going in; I have always averted my gaze and pretended I didn't know what was coming. But that only meant the sharp, piercing sensation was always a shock. My lip involuntarily trembled as he poked the tender and fleshy part of my gum. The orthodontist called me a brave girl. You whisper over, and over, that I am okay, I am okay, I am okay, as you deliver that punctuating intrusion.

I am laid out biblically over the mattress. The heels of your hands are pressing mine above my head, and your knees keep my legs pinned in place. You have martyred me in my own bed. There is a rushing sensation in my blood, like everything inside me is rising upwards and leaving through my skin.

Your gluttony collects on my chest and at my stomach. It pools in my belly button and slides off of me onto the sheets. Rolling over, you pat your full stomach and wipe the leftovers dripping from your mouth. I bury myself under layer after layer of cinnamon-incense-scented linen, sinking into the hot soil of my sheets, waiting for my warmth to return to me; but I remain just as cold as you.

2.   The Death and the Rebirth

From our place on the mattress, you can see through my bedroom windows. Tonight, there is a tapestry of constellations, and in the morning, there will be perfect cotton-puff clouds and the very blue sky, and the early morning sun will make everything warm again.

There is some heavy, immovable thing at the bottom of my stomach. It weighs me down so that I am submerged into the mattress, the bed will have an impression of me when I rise; my feet tightly pressed together, arms folded over each other as I squeeze myself closed. I am scared of disturbing you by moving, the recent chill has turned my body stiff and creaky. When I shift, every bone groans and clicks into place. So, I stay painfully still.

When I close my eyes, all I can picture is you, red-flushed and golden against the blank canvas of my sheets. There is no sight like it. I think I must have dreamed you up, you are a perfect vision.

My teeth ache like they are being twisted and pulled out, and when I wipe my tongue over them, I half expect to feel red, raw gum instead. My stomach has resolved itself to a new greediness, a vacuous hunger, and everything echoes. My sweet boy, honey-dipped, spiced and saccharine, the thought of you melts against my tongue. I want to take you in! I want to swallow you whole! I want to keep you inside . . .

You roll over, and a bright light illuminates the back of your head and casts a harsh white halo. My angel, my angel. A violent pantomime rises and falls in my chest with each of your long, wind-up inhales and gentle, unfolding exhales. I wonder if you have fallen asleep.

I do not think I can sleep. I do not feel like I can ever sleep again. The same frantic thoughts turn over and over again in my mind, in perfect tempo with the click . . . click . . . click . . . *will you love me now?*—click—*could you still love me now?*—click—*please, please love me now*—click. I promise to be good. I promise to be glad. I promise to be grateful.

I am ravenous, hungry and helpless. Finally, I move, peeling myself off the sheets to reach for my nearby water bottle, performing an internal baptism. There is no stain on the sheets. I had almost forgotten there should be one. You have drawn out everything bloody, full-bodied and beating. There was nothing left to leave on the linens; you took it all from me.

3. The Stake/Turned

Since you left, I have taken up a hobby. There is a book that I keep on the nightstand. It is about a woman who feels like a voyeuristic intruder in the interiors of her own desire. No matter how ardently she tries, she is too illusory and fragmented to be wholly true or devotedly earnest. I pencilled, *I think I was made to love,* on the first page margin. A wishful admission fading out into the page.

The room looks different now that you have been inside it, smaller somehow, hollowed-out and cavernous. I have taken to filling the space. I have found that I starve better in company. Although all my guests get chewed up and spat out in the end. This place is a trap; in here, love is lured, ensnared, and digested. A part of them always stays behind, circling and roaming when my eyes are closed. The phantom moans used to scare me, but they sound a bit like music now.

I had been desperate for you to stay, even erecting altars in your biblical reverence. The abrasive iconography of your paintings on my wall and the photos of you on my mirror. How long could I have kept you tempted with these ostentatious testaments to your vanity? My devotion, your trophy. Did you feel flattered to see yourself, so warm and alive?

My body is repenting you. On some cosmic level, it has recognised you as a great spiritual evil, an insidious intrusion, and has taken to discharging you in thick white clumps. There is a new odour to my flesh, the smell of rotting wood.

In this tomb, the same thoughts oscillate in my mind. I think I was made for love to move through. I think I was made to hold love in my hands and watch it slip through the seams of my fingers. I think I was made to host love, to let love kick up its feet and rest from a long journey.

I am restless, starved and forlorn. But, there is always someone to keep you fed, and full, and happy; someone else to bleed.

—ANGEL SYLVIA (she/her)

September

Meredith breathes in the muddy lake and scrunches her nose. The argil smell is stale and pungent, and Meredith can't decide if it's always been that way.

"What's a summer?" she thinks. It isn't this place. These stony beaches and lake edges so close she swears if she got enough zip behind it, she could throw a stone across the span of the water.

What's La Jolla?

Some chintzy sun-faded stucco in bubble gum? Days spent sun-sick and delirious, but somewhere different.

Somewhere new.

The feel of the sand left in her shoes. The smell of food braised with soy sauce and Sprite. A glut of faces all varied and dizzyingly unique. The faithful hush of an ocean she never knew could look and feel so infinite spread before her. That sense that everything is more. So much more than home.

And there the question sits since she got back: What is home?

Meredith gets up from the metal bench beneath the pavilion, takes her shoes off, and starts down the hill toward the shore of Long Branch Lake, thinking about home. Half-way down, she passes the lake's only bathroom, reeking of piss and lake water. It has no roof, and walls barely taller than she. Some ten feet from the bathroom entrance, a trio of spouts to wash off the lake muck and sand are in use. There are two people there. A mother and a child.

Meredith likes the pair together, and as she makes her way down toward them, they see Meredith. She smiles and takes a wide berth to get past.

"Day's mostly done," the drawl of the voice is long and raspy. The mother is smiling at Merideth when she says it.

"You from these parts?" Meredith laughs. "Born 'n raised," the mother says.

"Me too."

That's not right. Meredith knows everyone here. It's hard not to in their little prairie town. "Left when I was probably your age," the mother presses the button below the spout where her son continues to rinse off, "damn near a lifetime ago I figure."

"Your people still here?" A nagging feeling begins to eat away at Meredith. Something about the mother, but she can't make sense of it. As if she can see the mother with her son, she can take the word "mother" and affix it to the woman before her, but it isn't quite right.

"They're around, yeah. You know the Dunns?"

"You mean ol' Mr. Dunn and Patty," Meredith asks, "Those Dunns?" The mother nods, "That's them."

It's all off. Meredith can feel it looking at this stranger. Anxious energy pushing the button on the shower, hair pulled back tight and cinched through the opening of her baseball cap dyed a sun-washed daisy.

"Yeah, left when I was eighteen," the mother says it more to herself while looking past the beach toward the water, "lake's still pretty like I remember."

The mother leans against the shower pole, bearing her weight on her back leg as she taps her other foot. She wears an unpretentious pair of canvas plimsolls in white.

"Do you actually miss it?" Meredith scoffs.

The mother turns back and presses the button on the water spout again and the boy howls in delight, "I figure it's still home," she pauses as if surprised she's admitting it, "Maybe like part of me still ain't left."

Merideth spots a golden line of jewelry caressing an ankle, brown and devoid of tan lines. Something about it makes her blush when she sees it. She registers the image just before the boy starts flinging water in every direction, thrashing like a pig in mud.

Translucent strands of blond hair cling to the boy's head, creating a part straight down the middle that frames the edges of his face. Every few seconds, two tusks of ivory flash from under his lips. He gnashes the water, biting down so hard the snap of his teeth causes the muscles at the base of Merideth's skull to tighten. His face is plump and red with childhood brutishness. The boy catches Meredith frowning at him and grins.

The boy bends his knees as another blast of water rains down. It only takes Merideth following the toothy menace to understand: a golden stream sputters out from the bottom of the boy's swim trunks hitting his knees, shins, and bare feet. Meredith grimaces and looks towards the mother hoping she's noticed; the mother returned to gazing across the quivering sheet of glass at the unbroken wall of rocks and foliage cradling the lake from the other side. The boy yanks a towel off his parent's shoulder to dry himself when she doesn't move to press the spout.

And there, glowing underneath terry cloth, the mother's bare shoulders outlined against the lake and tree line behind her. Delicately traced and freckled in golden brown, the umber skin of the mother's shoulders curves inward forming the frame of her collarbone. Meredith sucks in her breath following the nape of the mother's neck up to her jaw and then to her ears; a single, exquisite line. To see it so carelessly—a sybaritic, elegant formation of flesh and muscle. The ease, the second nature of it all, sets Merideth's face, then her body, on fire. The woman turns back to Meredith, lips parted in a beckoning half-smile,

"Do me a favor, hun,"

***

The beach is manmade: a mélange of lake bed stones and pebbles mixed with silt and then mixed again with clay from the lake, covers what used to be a stony alcove.

It's certainly not La Jolla.

Meredith keeps toying with the idle thought. She pictures the ocean again, and the beaches, and eternal boardwalks and tries to ignore the hems and haws of the boy sitting next to her.

"When's she coming back?" he asks without an ounce of uncertainty. Meredith shrugs, "Dunno, soon. She isn't gonna leave you."

The son, Wally, picks up a smooth stone and stands up next to Meredith to survey the beach. Most of the visitors have already packed and gone. What's left are the miserable few too day-drunk to leave when they still had legs to. Meridith, then Wally, see a man wobbling back to his car after a day of poor fishing.

"Don't even think about it," Meredith says as soon as Wally sets himself flat-footed in the sand like a pitcher.

164

"Think about what?" Wally feigns a sincere tone then winds up and whips the rock at the drunk coming up the beach. It grazes left just missing the man's head, before hitting the water and cutting on the surface and out of sight. The man doesn't break stride, he walks as if Wally hadn't nearly embedded a rock into his unsuspecting forehead.

Meredith grabs Wally by one of his ankles and yanks the boy's leg out from under him. His back thuds into the sand next to her and he makes the sort of noise that sounds like lungs being deflated.

"You're a little cretin, you know that?" Meredith tries to sound angry.

Between barks of air returning to his lungs and an infectious cackle, Wally rolls from side to side ignoring Meredith.

She smiles in spite of herself. Wally's brutish charm is just that, charming, "You always get away with stuff like this, you little shit?"

Meredith takes a handful of sand and squashes it into Wally's hair, Wally howls like he did at the water spout.

"Can I go?" He asks when the laughing recedes and he cleans the sand from his hair. "I dunno," Meredith answers, "you could, I guess."

Thinking of the pang of hunger she felt seeing Wally's mother against the backdrop of the lake Meredith asks, "Does your mom do this a lot?"

Wally shrugs, "Not really, but I know people think she's weird back home." "Where's home?"

Wally spits a bit of sand and snorts something up into the back of his throat and swallows, "California."

Is that it? The effortless air of sensual detachment? The energy, the playfulness. The beauty. Like someone perfectly themself and more.

"Where in California?"

Wally scans the beach searching for something, "Oxnard."

Her hopes dampen hearing a name she's never heard before, but Meredith follows up, "Is that near La Jolla?"

Wally shakes his head, "I don't know what La Jolla is."

A strip of land made of limestone and clay juts into the lakefront, neatly dividing the beach into two sections: where Meredith and Wally are sitting on the beach and the slipway. The jetty extends nearly a hundred yards into the lake, and at its very tip, Wally and Meredith transfix on a lone figure standing in the waning afternoon facing the water.

"Can I go now?"

"Your mom said she'd come get you," Even as she's saying it, Meredith doesn't know why she agreed to watch Wally in the first place.

Why would she say yes?

Because of the way she grinned at Meredith. Because of the way she said it.

"Do me a favor, hun," like she was sharing a secret with Meredith. Some unspoken agreement that doing so would make it clear to Meredith why she's enthralled by the mother in the first place.

The pair don't notice the drunk approach. The shadow of an unsteady posture darkens out the sun and Wally and Merideth look up to see a dirty face and a pair of eyes incapable of focusing. Meredith shoots up and grabs Wally by the arm, pulling him behind her.

"You need something, mister?"

"Wha—" the fisherman hiccups and squares his shoulders. Wally giggles from behind as the two watch the drunkard try to steady his head.

Meredith takes a step back with Wally, balls her free hand into a fist, "Mister, I'm gonna ask nicely, best be on your way."

Wally can't stop laughing through his teeth and Meredith can feel him try to stifle the body tremors running through him. The fisherman squints then lets out a soft burp,

"Bah fin, just trinen'get home."

Meredith and Wally step to one side, "Sounds good, mister," she says.

The drunk waves his hand as if shooing away the pair, "Never—" the fisherman stutters and burps, then with a sudden grimace, he retches the afternoon from his stomach at Merideth's feet.

"Gross," Wally yells in complete enjoyment as Meredith curses under her breath. "Better now," the fisherman hiccups and grins before he starts back toward the hill stepping in the mush and gummy stew of sour beer and deli meats, past Meridith, towards whatever he calls home. He turns to the two still dumbfounded by the vomit, and tips a hat he isn't wearing.

"This place rules," Wally says, "People here are so weird. Nobody's this fun back home."

"Fun," Meredith is looking down at the spatter of vomit staining her pants, "You're not from here, it's only fun because you're a tourist."

Wally picks up another stone from the sand and hands it to Meredith, "Whatever, bet you can't hit him before he gets up the hill."

The fisherman is just starting up the slope toward the parking lot overlooking the beach.

It's not a steep hill, but one could assume after a day of heavy drinking, the slope feels as treacherous as K2. Meredith rubs the smooth lakestone between her thumb and index finger thinking with enough zip, she could hit him. But why would she do that?

Because Wally, like his mother, is different. From this place, from these people, from Meredith. Because throwing the rock would be funny, and different, and something she would do if she wasn't from here—she was a tourist like them. Maybe, just for a second she can be from somewhere else. Meredith plants herself to throw the stone at the man inching his way up the slope when a raspy drawl breaks her concentration, "Wally give you any guff?"

Meredith turns to see Wally's back racing toward his mother. She is glowing against the twilight and Meredith doesn't know if the mother is real. Wearing the same half-smile, she seems more an apparition until she scoops up Wally for a hug and makes her way toward Meredith.

Meredith looks back at the fisherman to find him in nearly the same place, and lets the stone fly. It arcs high before coming straight down on the man and hitting him in the small of his back. He doesn't notice and continues his journey as if nothing outside of the step he took and the one he's about to take is present in his world.

Wally howls again, and his mother makes her way to Meredith, "He has a way, don't he?" Meredith isn't thinking about Wally though, "Why'd you leave?"

The mother gives a thoughtful look, "Thought I needed more, I guess."

"Do you ever think about coming back for good?"

The mother smiles a different smile at the question and shakes her head, "Too much time, too much change. Still, sometimes it feels like the lake still got a magic in it."

Meredith has a sense she isn't saying anything here has changed, and that seems a small tragedy to her. Like losing something precious but not remembering what it is or how you lost it. It leaves an indelible absence.

She doesn't wait for Meredith to respond.

"You know, before that poor man who got chewed up by the motorboat, I used to swim to the other shore when the sun went down." She's wistful, almost mournful, "Back when this was home."

Meredith perks up, opens her mouth, then frowns, "Why would you swim to the other shore?

The mother smiles, "You never been?"

She doesn't answer Meridith's question, instead, she turns to her impish son and holds her hand out to leave.

Wally bears his teeth up at Meredith as he follows his mother, "I told you this place rules."

The pair passes the fisherman just before he reaches the top and then disappear over the crest of the hill, leaving Meredith with her thoughts and the silent lake of magic. She wades ankle deep into the lake water, thinking she prefers the calm of it to the anxious pull of the Pacific tide.

"Home."

The word slipping past her lips and into the air makes the empty beach feel less lonely.

***

Meredith can't stop thinking about what the mother said; maybe there is magic in a place like this, or maybe magic is just an approximation. Either way, she decides to head out to the jetty where she and Wally watched that solitary visage of the mother and wondered what it was that compelled her to leave her son with a stranger.

Standing at the edge of the jetty, Meredith tries to breathe deep and take the brown magic lake in. She listens for the water to speak. For the wind to whisper. For anything, really. The lake doesn't move, shifting lazily against the rocky outcropping as if to shrug at Meredith's expectation for something more. She picks up another stone, flat and smooth, winds up, and flings it across the water. It skips once before it plops into the water and disappears.

You've never been? She hears the words repeat. What could be there? More clay and woods? Leaves just like the ones on the trees on this side? Human debris left inert for decades, slowly disintegrating back into the marrow of the earth? From the jetty, the other shore is vague and blurry, and Merideth guesses at least a quarter mile from where she's standing. It couldn't really be anything other than that, could it?

Maybe the magic is in the water.

Meredith doesn't think past the first thought, she just jumps headfirst with the easy grace of a child raised to swim. She breaks the surface and kicks out as far as she can hold her breath. She opens her eyes beneath water and finds she wades through an undulating haze. Extending her arms in a breaststroke, Meredith cuts through the brown veil of silt and clay as if passing through some ephemeral nowhere. She doesn't notice the breath in her lungs as she swims further and deeper. She doesn't know how long she's been at it before the need to breathe feels like she'll die if she doesn't. Meredith breaches the water, gasping and alive.

It doesn't make sense.

The jetty must be more than two hundred yards away from her. Meredith is exactly halfway between the beach where she met Wally and his mother and the other side of the lake. Could she have gotten that far? She looks across the remaining span of the lake toward the other side.

"Why not?" Meredith says.

Turning away from the beach and jetty where she came, Meredith continues on toward the other side of the lake, wondering if the path she traces is the same one the mother took in some era where everything was sepia-toned and hazy.

Fen, morass, wetland, bog—she keeps searching for words that fit better than lake. Swamp is too obvious. Bog seems too mean-spirited, but calling it a lake feels too close to calling it an ocean. As if this place shares something with the shores of the Pacific—it doesn't. Swimming in its bosom, Meredith is at least sure of that distinction. The odor of it, the sting, and earthiness make Meridith think of mud, primordial and untouched sitting deep at the bottom of an ancient trench.

She pictures a torso she saw once several summers ago when she was slight and couldn't understand what she was seeing then: flesh split vertically at the waist up to the base of a pale throat, lifeless and open. Were there innards, or organs?—She can't remember. A sodden mass of flesh dragged out of the lake by trawl. An accident, a family, mourners, and lookers-on covering their mouths and shielding their faces when they see it too. Weird and tragic to be sure, but home nonetheless.

"Home," she says it like there's an alchemy to uttering those sounds in this place. As if she's conjuring some part of that body disintegrated into chum and lake muck, and willing it to show her something. She is met with nothing more than the sound of her arms crashing against the water and the stillness of a summer at its end.

When she reaches the far shore, Meredith drags herself, clothes sopping and heavy, to the nearest patch of warm earth and collapses into the ground. She is asleep before her head hits the sand.

****

Her skin is stippled and freezing in the white glow of the moon. There are no clouds overhead. A blanket of gaseous light bears down on her in quiet expectation. She feels her toes, burning and cold, then her feet kicking in the darkness. Then a jolt of blood biting her fingers, her chest, and finally her cheeks.

Meredith squirms up to her elbows then sits upright in damp sand on a stretch of embankment on the farthest edge south of Long Branch Lake. The jetty where she dove headlong into the water is a pencil-thin line obscured by darkness at the farthest reaches of what she makes out in the moonlight.

She is freezing and tired and only now realizing how careless she's been while trying to figure out how not to die of exposure. And there, folded next to her: dry clothing, socks, and a pair of shoes. Overcome with cold, and with what feels like an automatic physiological response, Merideth strips herself down to nothing. No towel, but the air, even as late as it is, feels pleasant enough that warmth rushes into her as she strips away each waterlogged piece of cloth. Her skin is glowing and nearly pearlescent standing against the black lake. Reaching down for the first piece of clothing she can find, Meredith's gaze levels against the still water, infinitely serene and unmoved by her presence. She does not sense something lurking just beneath the surface, or as though somewhere unseen, a set of glowing eyes watch her like prey. No, the feeling that creeps into her is one she only associates with the sort of anxious divinity she felt looking at the rolling tide of the ocean receding back past the horizon. An almost abject serenity bound in isolation and terror as though the impenetrable lake has taken her as its own.

But why? Why is she here now, standing at the water's edge stripped bare like a newborn?

Because she's never been.

A voice, not her voice and not a voice from within; a woman's voice, clear and forbearing. Meredith tries to make out the words, if there are any, but the voice pulls back passing behind her towards a thicket of trees through the forest at her back. She for an instant nearly turns to follow the voice into the dark, but remembers her nakedness. Standing on the lakeshore nude and freezing, Merideth instead reaches for the pile of dry clothing folded neatly at her feet.

A cotton pullover, whose color is indistinguishable in the moonlight. From what Merideth can discern, it is heavy and fleece-lined. When she feels the fabric on her skin, she is hit with the rush of safety and comfort that only comes from trying on new clothes for the first time, magnified by the fact that she was not fully aware of how cold she actually was before she put the sweater on. Meredith then picks up the pair of dry pants folded along with the sweater: denim, not unlike what she was wearing before. She slides her legs into the jeans, and they fit like a miracle. She pulls up the socks stuffed individually with each shoe and finally notices the shoes.

A pair of white plimsolls.

Finally, Meredith turns to face the tree line set back against the far end of the shore. The dogwood and maple give her nothing but the occasional sigh at the moonlight breeze.

"Hello?"

There is no answer. Meredith waits a beat then tries again.

"Is anyone there?" Her stomach sinks with each second that passes undisturbed. She is uneasy in the silence, not from fear, but more a wild compulsion to know. She calls out again, "You can come out."

At once, just at the edge of her periphery Merideth catches something. Movement, but as she turns her head to look the movement seems like moonlight creeping between the shadows of leaves and branches. Then, maybe a hundred or so feet into the trees, the light moves glowing—passing from one spot to another. The motion is deliberate, living.

Still, Merideth can't make out what it is exactly. She forces herself to inch closer to the light. Little by little, Meredith makes it to the back edge of the shore, bracing up against the forest. She thinks first to step into the darkness in hopes of following the light, but something about the thought feels wrong. Not wrong in that reptilian way, but as if to cross the threshold of the trees would be profane. Like she is violating something sacred. So, Merideth leans up against a sturdy maple that peeks out of the natural border of the forest and tries to focus on following the moving light.

To her horror, there is something—after a minute passes of Merideth straining to penetrate the bramble and separate the natural dance of the forest for something "other", she sees it. In full view, cutting between a large clearing of trees and low bushes, walking away from her—further into the darkness. Light, gray, and at first, formless.

Delicate shoulders covered at their points by a gown, flaxen, nearly translucent hair braided to the waist. The shape of a head held slightly tilted up. The figure doesn't bob or sway as it moves further away—it floats, gliding. Meredith's breath catches in her tongue and teeth, and the space around her heart tightens as she begins to shiver. She tries to fight back the spasm rolling through her body as she watches the figure disappear and reappear among the dogwoods and maples. She hears it again. Something like a voice, perfect and almost soothing.

"I see you." it seeps into her mind and sinks down into her stomach as her legs give out.

Meredith slumps against the tree, her vision darkening. The soil around the tree is soft and inviting, and Meredith's body completely submits to exhaustion nestled in the hollow of roots and grass. The woods fade from her mind and as they do, the gray light, soft shoulders, and braided flax fade also into black repose.

***

Incessant, staccato trilling wakes her, or at least pulls her mind out from the depths of heavy sleep. Merideth lifts herself not from the hollow of the tree, but once from the sands of the very beach where everything transpired the day before.

She greets the misty lake before her and is met with an affable silence. An equally drowsy sun causes a sheet of delicate mist to rise from the lake's surface—it is sluggish like the rest of the morning. As though the day is trying to wake itself; slowly yes, but surely. Still out of sight, and far enough off, the angry braying of fishing boat motors are swallowed up by the nothing of morning air.

Lost in her wondering about whether anything really happened the night before, or if she is just waking from some heat induced fever dream, a cicada song reverberates into Meredith's ears somewhere among overgrown weeds and damp lake soil. She feels it slither down her spine. As real as it's ever been.

The sun is still hidden somewhere low and far away, but the day has started. The sky is obstructed by clouds that smell like rain waiting just beneath Meredith's nose. She can hear the low rumble of cars and semis coming and going somewhere south of where she is, Highway 36. She is so close to home, she hadn't realized she could hear from the lake if she had ever thought to listen. Getting up, still dressed in the clothes she found the night before, Merdith follows the footsteps back up the hill the way Wally, his mother, and the drunk all went.

Towards the white hum of morning traffic. Towards her still-sleeping town, immutable and now more exasperating than it's ever been. Home, towards mangled streets and sober edifices stirring restless, their voices reaching Meridith through dust and ash. She is hearing them for the first time and can't help but muse,

"This place rules."

—LW PLATT (he/him)

It starts with her shoulder.

One morning, she wakes to find it gleaming—not sweating, not wet, but gleaming. The skin has gone clear. Light filters through it like pond water through a jar. When she knocks, it makes a sound like distant windchimes. She doesn't knock again.

By noon, the transparency has spread to her clavicle. Her pulse is still visible, but it's a whisper now, twitching like a shy animal. Her mother doesn't notice. Her mother never looks at the part of her that's leaving.

She eats soup for dinner and watches it slide down her throat, the heat fogging the glass. Her sister calls her a freak, but only when she thinks no one's listening. It echoes anyway.

The doctor says it might be psychological. "Like anorexia, or eczema," he offers. She wants to ask how a thought turns into glass, but she is afraid of his answer.

By bedtime, her lips are slick and reflective. She kisses her own palm and cuts it open.

The blood looks like berries in snow.

In school, she stops speaking. Her voice sounds wrong to her—too soft, like it might shatter the ribs from the inside. Her best friend, Mira, sends her a note folded into a heart:

"Are you okay? You seem see-through."

She doesn't answer. How do you say: *Yes, I am, literally.*

Her teacher marks her present but never calls on her. Her desk is moved near the window. Maybe they think sunlight helps. It doesn't. It only shows the air bubbles forming in her arms—delicate imperfections, like trapped breath.

By Friday, her legs are glass too. Walking makes a tiny clinking sound, like someone stirring sugar into a teacup. Her mother buys her new slippers.

"To keep the cold out," she says, not looking directly at her.

The doctor prescribes silence and supervised solitude.

"It could reverse," he says, but she hears *rehearse*. As if she's practising absence. As if becoming nothing takes discipline.

The glass reaches her eyes on a Sunday.

When she cries, the tears clink softly—glass on porcelain—before resting like pearls in the sink. She keeps them in a jar by her bed. Proof she still feels.

One night, Mira climbs through the window and finds it. Her fingers hover, hesitant.

"You're not a freak," she whispers. "You're . . . like a cathedral no one prays in anymore."

The girl almost says, *Exactly*. But instead, she leans in and kisses Mira's wrist.

The glass doesn't cut this time.

It sings.

By morning, her shoulder has turned warm again.

—KEERTHANA NALAMOTHULA (she/her)

LOS CEMPASÚCHILES

*the ancestors always pass down
gifts—just open your hand
and trust the natural world.*

"You're here . . . *again?*"

"If you ain't realized by now, we don't always get what we want," remarks Esa, the self-proclaimed leader. "Has Momma taught you anything, *chica?*"

Yeah, they have. The real question is—

"What do you want now?"

"Your acknowledgement would be a great start."

I roll my eyes. *I can't acknowledge you . . . you are a goddamn—*

"People already judge me for *what* I am, I don't need them thinking that I'm some looney too," I hiss through a whisper, my eyes narrowing at the translucent vase of marigolds sitting idly on Nana's *chisme* table—the headquarters of gossip between the women of my family. Ironic setting for a thing so beautiful.

Esa rolls her eyes right back at me. She's the abrasive one of the marigolds, along with the tallest. I'd also like to tell you that she's the most vivid, although Lunita may be offended by that. "You still find yourself caring what people think?"

"Why wouldn't she?" Lunita says, her leaves crossing themselves.

"Es importante que intentemos comprenderla. Mierda, Esa, no es como si no fueras un complaciente de la gente en su día," Marisol says. She's normally bashful when it comes to Esa starting in on me, but maybe the sun got to her today.

Or maybe you've just lost your damn mind.

I offer her a thin smile. She reminds me of a few ancestors that still blossom in my memory, despite their entrance in the Spirit World long ago. Vivid manifestation, Spanish tongue—a reincarnation of the past, cultivation of everything that created me.

Lunita grins. She thinks she's slick.

176

Esa never likes being challenged by the other marigolds, but this time she concedes with an eye roll.

A few moments pass by under the Valley sunset. The three marigolds talk among themselves while I stare off into the abyss of summer. Mosquito hawks begin peopling the front lawn, while the trees groove to the rhythm of the breeze. These are the kind of evenings that have sustained me, even during the most daunting periods when everything felt like one big shitshow.

Mami emerges from our *casita*, Mijo in pursuit behind her. His small, chunky lugs move with haste, his *pucheros* painting his lips. "*¡Mami, no me dejes! ¡No me dejes!*"

"*Ay Mijo, necesito ir a la tienda. Mete tu culito en la ducha,*" she waves him off, before turning to me. "*Mija, asegúrate de que se bañe. Voy a la tienda a comprar ingredientes para la cena. Estaré en casa en un rato. Cierra la puerta, ¿vale?*"

I nod.

Mijo continues to whine, but relents once Mami raises her voice. I'm zoned out when that happens—*I tend to disconnect when voices raise. It reminds me of things I'd rather not dwell on.* Once I hear the ignition start, I look up at Mijo. His lips are still pouty and the rims of his eyes are moist.

"*¡Mami nos deja! ¡Mami nos deja!*"

"No she ain't," I stand up. "*Mami va a la tienda. Ahora ve a ducharte, cochino.*"

Mijo is reluctant to listen, yet he does anyway. *Gracias, Dios.*

When he's back inside, I glance at the marigolds. Observant eyes, they have, just as advanced as their manifestation. The sun sets upon them now, radiating them like candles we pray to every Sunday. *La luz para guiar a nuestros antepasados.*

Lunita is too busy enthralled by her Secret, Marisol is whispering her evening prayers, and Esa is staring off into oblivion. I shake my head and proceed to our *casita*, shutting the door behind me. *I AM NOT CRAZY, I SWEAR TO GOD!*

After I close the door behind me, I hear the shower turning on. I sigh in relief, grateful that I don't have to be the typical big sister and give my brother hell. Mami does enough of that. Good reason or not, I know what it's like to be nagged at—and I wish that I had someone growing up who could've reduced the nagging for me. *Oh, don't I wish for many things.*

While my brother showers, I head into the room Mami and I share. I take my phone from my back pocket and set it on the charger. My initial intention is to then lay down for a few moments, put my brain on a well-deserved pause. But rather, I find myself entering a vortex.

A *DON'T YOU DENY, YOU LITTLE GODDAMN—*

"*¿Cuánto tiempo planeas vivir una mentira?*"

You're just hearing things, you big fool. You're already on edge, what the hell do you REALLY expect at this point, chica?

"*Ay chavalla, sé que puedes escucharme.*"

I gingerly raise my head and see nothing. *Delusions, delusions, delusions.* I take a seat on my bed and rest my hands in my lap.

"What do you want?"

You always ask questions, even when answers seem far, far away.

"*El secreto, Chiquita. ¿Qué pasa con eso?*"

"*También puedes hablar conmigo en inglés, ¿sabes?*"

"*¿Por qué? ¿Eres una chica de No Sabo?*"

"*Soy Chicana.*" I'm prouder than I intend to be. "I was raised Chicana, not on some traditional shit."

The voice chortles, "There's been some dysfunction since I left, huh?"

"Something like that."

"Well, it's a shame that I'm not interested in the Dysfunction—my *chicas* already have me up to decent speed—"

I look around the room again, this time with even more scrutiny. *I will find the culprit of this voice. I will find the—*

"What are you?"

"Hm?"

I stare into the empty hallway, my eyes vigorous with a brewing apprehension. I hope it isn't as apparent as I anticipate, but Mami has always said I'm strong with emotional projection, especially in my face.

I sigh and repeat, "What. *Are.* You."

I come off strong, which I suppose surprises The Voice.

It releases a nervous laugh, then states, "I am only what you wish to be."

SHEISFREE. SHEISFREE. SHEISFREE.

I'm trippin' out, I'm trippin' out, I'M TRIPPIN—

"What are you talking about?"

"Look outside."

I can't explain the movement I'm doing now—it's a contrast between a leap and sprint. In a matter of moments I'm before those marigolds again. I don't even remember pulling myself from the bed, but I'm here. There's no time for questions or concerns. I need to find out what this is and what is happening.

I grab fistfuls of my abundant hair and look down at the marigolds.

Esa is still eyeing the sunset. Lunita is looking at Her still, with pensive eyes of admiration and desire. Marisol acknowledges me.

"*Estás de vuelta rápidamente.*"

This gathers the attention of the other two.

"I just got Mijo settled, that's all."

Esa glances at me, raises her observing eye, and winks. "Did you hear It?"

My jaw clenches. "Hear what?"

Marisol suddenly looks uneasy. "Esa—"

"*¡Cállate!*" She shakes. "Marisol, I will handle this."

As if talking marigolds ain't the craziest shit I've seen . . .

Lunita is still remaining silent, but the glint in her eye is vacant. She looks at the ground, gulping. *This can't be good.*

I feel the vortex thickening—so many things spinning fast, coherence diminishing. I can't put it into words or articulate a thing. I am . . .

"The truth," Esa stands tall among the three marigolds, confident. She looks like a *jefa*. "Or did you not get there yet?"

"I—"

"It takes one crazy thing to know another, *chavalla.*"

A tear rolls down my cheek.

"What is going on?"

"You are what you fear . . . "

"E-Esa-"

"Take hold of me, please."

"E-Esa, *p-por favor-*"

"Marisol!"

My hand obeys and I take that marigold in my trembling hand.

***

Many years later

"And that's how I knew I was . . . Well, *different.*"

My granddaughter holds the dried marigolds and offers me a sympathetic look.

Maritza must've told her already that I'm looney. Shit.

"Do you think they'll do the same for me?"

Oh?

"The same?"

"Tell me the truth, that is," my *mija* wonders, twirling her curly brown hair. "Do you think it'll tell me if I"m different, too?"

"There's only one way to find out."

180

She grabs ahold of the marigolds.

Then, the ancestors deliberate in the Spirit World.

—M.S. BLUES (she/her)

My aunt told me the woman's late husband was buried in the field behind her house, and each day she was wishing him good morning and good night. At school, the girls who hung out in the handicapped stall smoking out the vent told me she was strung out on drugs, completely zombified. They said she'd killed her husband in a mad fit and consumed him bit by bit, and when finally she ate his brain, she lost it for good. One summer, when my little cousins came from the city to stay for a month while their parents finalized divorce papers, my mom told them the woman was on the lookout for bad spirits, and made sure we kept our distance so she could continue her vital guardianship uninterrupted.

But I know better.

Since I had been old enough that my whereabouts were not always accounted for, I had been visiting the short, wide, pale pink house that the woman lived in. I first went out of the morbid curiosity that drives kids to find the limits of what is safe and allowed. I snuck around the house, that was perched at the end of Merrymount Road which wound through town, past the school, the grocer's, narrowing up the gentle slope south of town that delivered on to our house—and the houses of most of the people who lived beyond the town limits—and finally terminated in the driveway to the woman's house. There was a vast meadow behind her house that butted up against a creek which eventually fed into the Tillamook River. I crept through the tall grass, carving an arc that gradually approached the far back corner of the house, which I had deduced was her sitting room.

On that first day, I spotted her shuffling between a set of built-in shelves stuffed with books and an oval, dark wood table, carrying sets of papers in yellowed plastic bins, doing the sort of menial organizing my parents did after I went to bed sometimes when their voices would get tense like they were on the same side of an argument with some third, mute entity. This endeared her to me. I watched for most of the afternoon. The grass around me became matted or else plucked up and replaced by my idle hands. I took breaks from my post to strip down and cool off in the creek and to follow a trail of ants to where they descended down a crevice in the dry earth.

Upon returning to check on her after a break sunbathing with some lizards, I found her staring out her window directly at me. I flattened to my belly like someone had swiped my legs out from under me, but her gaze was uninterrupted, looking past where I had been standing, past the creek and the thick grove of young oaks beyond it. Cautiously, I crawled closer, cutting diagonally across the meadow to escape the beam of her eyes. I got close enough that I could see the cinder block skirting around the house and almost jumped at the feeling of the rubber garden hose coiled up under my forearm as I slithered up. The sun was low by then, and much of the window was ablaze with its reflection, but by shifting just so, I was able to position a dark spot in the reflection over her face so that every detail of her came into view. I had never seen her this close before, and she was much younger than I expected, probably not much older than my own mom, although she seemed wearier and tougher, like blackberry thorns would break against her skin. And she was weeping. Leaking. Tears streamed down her face and her nose was running and her whole body was quivering and occasionally jolting like a wave up from her pelvis that whipped her neck first back then forward. Then suddenly, she collapsed and was out of sight. I rushed to the window and saw her convulsing on the ground and slammed my palms against the glass. Her eyes snapped up to mine and a bit of her immense sorrow was replaced by an inquisitive expression. It wasn't until she was opening the back door and inviting me in that I realized I was also crying. I wiped the tear streaks and my hand returned muddy from the dirt that had clung to my tears.

Inside, we both stood averting each other's eyes. I felt foolish and intrusive and was acutely aware of our age difference and stranger-ness.

Then, she asked, "Do your parents know where you are?"

I shifted a little and wiped my hands on my denim shorts. "They don't mind." It didn't occur to me that her question could've been a warning. Her pointing out that I had been caught in a stranger's backyard spying, and she, having the ability to inform my parents, was exercising that influence. But she seemed just as naïve to these implications, and asked in the same way one might ask a person from another country what they eat for dinner.

"Do you want a glass of water?"

"Yes, please. And thank you—and sorry too. I thought something was happening to you, like a seizure or some terrible thing."

She brought us water in blue glass cups and offered me cookies from a tin that she set on the oval table after shuffling some papers out of the way. She let me ask her a lot of questions and didn't dismiss them like people often did when the subject matter was death or money or why adults cry and yell. It got dark fast, and I had to excuse myself to race home. But the next day I came back, this time to the front door where she greeted me warmly and we sat and drank glasses of bitter iced tea and swatted flies away from a plate of apple slices.

I came back whenever I could. When school started again I came less frequently, and weeks would sometimes go by, but eventually neither of us worried about whether we'd see each other again, and I stopped fretting about any particular cadence. I would tell her things I couldn't tell anybody, like about the wine I stole from my parents and how my best friend and I kissed on a sleepover in 7th grade, and she seemed to not remember, but I got nervous every time I talked to her now about how much I stared at her lips and into her mouth and at her bottom molars when she laughed. And she told me everything she had to tell, and about how glad she was to have someone to talk to and that she knew about all the rumors around her, though she hadn't heard the one about guarding against bad spirits and she liked that one and joked that I should try to get it to catch on. She also told me about her husband, who was not dead, but had left her for a man he'd met on a dating site. I was in high school at this point and thought of my best friend's mouth, though we hadn't talked in over a year, and said, "That's awful."

"No, it wasn't." She looked for a long time at an ant crossing her knee. "We weren't like that." It turned out they had only gotten married because there had been rumors about both of them and at the time rumors of that sort could ruin your life. She laughed when she said that, because it had only changed what the rumors were about. They had also gotten married because she wanted a baby, and he had been happy to help. After years of trying, a doctor informed her that her ovaries were underdeveloped and she would never bear a child. Her husband left shortly after because he had nothing to offer her and the attitudes in cities had shifted enough that he thought it would be safe. He invited her to come with him, but she loved the country and this house and how the creek looked like lava when the late sun hit it.

I got angry when she told me this. "You made me feel completely alone." I called her a coward and didn't see her for a month, until I ran into her at the grocery store. I was lingering behind my mom while she shopped. It felt perverted to be around her in public with my mom there. We made eye contact and I started to cry and had to storm off to the bathroom. I stripped naked and felt the wetness between my legs in slow hard circles getting hotter until it could've melted rock and I had to clutch the sink as my abdomen seized and shuddered and I watched my face in the mirror contort through bleary eyes.

My second kiss happened during the fall of my freshman year at a state university several hours away, where I had received a scholarship to study architecture. I fell into an intense relationship with a girl I met who was from the town the college was in. She had a lot more experience than me and would tell me softly just how to touch her with my fingers and tongue and laugh when I asked for reassurance in a way that melted me more than her hot breath teasing my nipples or the underside of my thigh.

When summer came I went back home and got a job at a seasonal stand that sold ice cream cones and saran wrapped sandwiches near a popular beach on the lake west of town that someone filled in with white sand and that was replenished at the start of each summer by two big dump trucks. My girlfriend, as we had recently agreed to call each other, stayed in the university town with her parents. We called for hours a day and when we weren't talking I was missing her terribly, so everyone experienced me in a continually sour mood. I hadn't told anyone about her, and my parents thought my mood was a sign that university had somehow spoiled me to the beauty of our town. They commented often on how lucky I was that they left my room available to me instead of renting it out for some extra income which they could've really used. My expressions of gratitude did nothing to counteract these comments. On one occasion, when I said that dad could never stand having a stranger living in the house with them, mom asked if I was trying to get myself replaced by some rent-paying stranger. I cooked them dinner that night and did the dishes as well, and my mom played with my hair while we watched a rom-com that dad fell asleep to.

My parents went to bed when the movie ended and I put on a flannel and went outside to call my girlfriend. I called twice in a row with no answer, so I texted *free to call? <3*, and meandered down the road waiting for a response. I found myself then at the end of Merrymount Road, confronting that squat house. I made to turn around but realized she was sitting on the front porch with a glass of white wine looking right at me like an owl. My phone began to buzz just then and I stood frozen, staring back, feeling my phone, unable to answer or move. She stood up and went into the house. I stood there while my phone stopped vibrating. When she came back out, she held a second glass and the bottle, which was cold and perspiring. I walked up the short drive and sat next to her. I finished my glass of wine before we exchanged words. As she filled my second glass, she asked, "Why didn't you ever come back?" and I looked from my glass to her. Her eyes were fixed on the pouring spout. Her mouth was slightly ajar and the center of her top lip was wet and glistening from the wine. I became hot all over. I couldn't bear to look higher than the divot at the base of her neck. I got up then, rushed into her house, and began grabbing books off her shelves and throwing them at the wall. I broke the vase full of dried peonies on the oval table and tore the flowers off their stems and stomped so hard my teeth clanged against each other and my knees hurt.

She stood in the doorway with her glass of wine in her hand and I swatted at it and it spilled all over her and I screamed *SLUT. DYKE. PERVERT. FAGGOT. COWARD.* I got in her face and spewed spit with each word. I screamed into her ear until we were both deaf. I smashed all the plates and bowls and cups and kicked my shoes off and tracked blood through her house and took off my flannel and ripped it to pieces and then my t-shirt.

She just stood there and eventually I was exhausted and my feet burned and I limped into her bedroom and curled into myself on her bed. I heard her come into the room and when she got in bed she reached her arms and legs around me and enveloped me. I turned around and pressed my face into her chest. She had undressed and put on an oversized t-shirt, and I could feel the softness of her skin through the thin fabric. I scooped my hands under her shirt and hooked them around her shoulders. Then I lifted her shirt and tucked myself into it. Her nipples were dark and hard and I rubbed them against my cheek and nose and heard myself cooing.

She stayed holding me and my hands came around and went up through the top hole of the shirt. I ran them up her neck and along the topography of her lips and cheeks and gently over her closed eyes and up into her hair. Then, I brought them down, tracing across her lips, first circling the outer rim then pressing into the space between her lower lip and her gums. I ran my finger along the tops of her teeth, pushing hard on her lower canines so her mouth opened wider, and I felt an indent left behind on my finger. Then to her molars and back along the inside of her cheek. She held me tighter with her legs and her pubic hair pressed wet against my belly. She rolled then so that she was on top of me, straddling, and she pulled her head in so we were both inside her massive t-shirt. It was warm and humid and smelled of grass and laundry detergent. All the stray bits of hair that had come out of her braid floated down and tickled my ears. One strand got caught in my open mouth and she brushed it away, along with my own hair that had become stuck to my cheek with sweat, and folded it all behind my ear. She brought her hands behind my back and unclasped my bra, pulling it off and out from our shirt tent. She reached down and undid the button to my pants and pulled my underwear off with them and we kept looking into each other's eyes. I shivered as the open air touched my inner thighs. We rolled onto our sides, facing each other. With her hands behind both my knees, she collected my legs up into the shirt and intertwined them with hers so that we were both entirely contained in the veil of the t-shirt. We laid until our blinks got longer and longer and we both drifted to sleep.

—JOSIE YACONELLI (she/her)

Low Tide

I only ever saw her at the low tide.

She'd be down by the rocks, just where the sand turned slippery and the barnacles cut if you weren't careful. She wore a long, dark coat that always looked wet, even when it hadn't rained. The first time I noticed her, she was crouched low on the biggest rock, the one shaped like a whale's back, with her chin tilted sideways toward the water, listening. She said something I couldn't catch. A soft murmur, broken by the wind.

Like someone caught halfway between a memory and a wave.

After that, I saw her most mornings. Always in the same coat, always near the same rock. She never walked too far—just along the tide-line, back and forth, like she was tracing something invisible. Sometimes she'd stop and speak aloud, but not the way people do when they're on the phone or muttering to themselves about groceries. Her voice floated like it wasn't meant for here. Like it belonged out past the horizon.

Mum told me to leave her alone.

"She's mourning," she said, like that explained everything.

But mourning looked different in books. Mourning wore black and cried in church pews, or held folded flags at graves. It didn't look like pacing the beach at dawn, asking questions to the wind. It didn't sound like calling someone who never answered back.

So I kept my distance.

I used to think she was mad—proper mad, the kind you're meant to stay away from. But one morning, just before the fog cleared, I saw something different.

The woman was sitting on the flattest rock, knees drawn up like she was bracing herself. Her coat was soaked past the dark hem, dragging on her. She held something small in her hands—a box.

A recorder, I'd learn later. But what struck me wasn't the object. It was the way she talked to it. Not like she was ranting.

Like she was confessing.

"If I could go back, I would've screamed louder," she whispered.

Then silence, even the sea knew when to hush.

The woman didn't cry. She looked like she wanted to—but she never did. She'd just sit there, stiff and still.

A statue that was left too close to the tide.

And then she'd ask things.

Strange, soft things.

"Did you hate me?"

"Are you waiting for me?"

She didn't want an answer, not really.

It wasn't mourning with black veils and graveyards. It was something messier. Like she missed someone, but also couldn't forgive herself for losing.

One morning, she wasn't there.

The tide rolled in, just like always, but the space where she usually stood was empty. The foam kissed the shore in gentle, rhythmic pulses, but there was no woman, no dark coat trailing behind her, no murmured questions drifting on the wind.

I didn't think much of it at first. Maybe she'd gotten tired of the beach. Maybe she was just sick of the sound of the sea.

So I waited. I played in the sand and kept an eye on the water.

But then the next morning came, and she wasn't there.

The morning after that, the beach was still bare.

Her absence was like a hole in the landscape. The sea kept crashing against the rocks, like it always did, but the usual quiet pressure that I felt when she was nearby was gone.

I strode along the shoreline, kicking the pebbles, searching the horizon.

Just the wind and the gulls.

Days passed.

Still nothing.

I asked Mum about her, but she just shook her head. "It's not our business," she said, her voice flat.

But it didn't feel like that. It felt wrong, like the world had shifted and I hadn't caught up yet.

I couldn't help myself. Even though something in my gut told me not to.

I searched the place where I'd seen her most.

And then, I saw it.

A small, grey object was half-buried near the boulders. At first, I thought it was a piece of driftwood, or maybe an old bottle washed up from the sea. But as I got closer, I could see it clearly: small, with cracked edges, but unmistakable.

A recorder, like the one Uncle Jim had when he worked on the ferries. The buttons were worn smooth. I turned it over in my hands.

Strange, heavy in the way objects felt when left behind. The play button stood out, scuffed. I hesitated, but the curiosity pulled me in.

I pressed it.

At first, it was just static, a soft, muffled hum, the kind of noise the sea made on a still day. Then, her voice.

Not like when she muttered along the waves, soft and disjointed, like the words carried away on the wind.

No, this was different. It was clearer, calmer. It wasn't the voice of someone lost in the pull of grief—it was sharper, more deliberate.

More like she was reading something she never sent.

"Do you think it was my fault?"

There was a long pause.

"Would you have told me if it was?" she asked, her voice barely a whisper, as if she was afraid of hearing the answer.

The questions went on. One after another, like she was speaking to someone she couldn't see. Most of them didn't make sense to me. Not in the way her words twisted.

Something about falling. About a promise. About her sister.

Her sister.

Was she the one the woman was grieving?

I almost stopped the recorder. I should've.

But then the last question came.

Her voice cracked. It broke a little.

"Do you remember what we promised, just before your fall?"

My finger hovered over the stop button, but it was too late.

A different voice—low and dark—answered her.

Not hers.

Not kind.

"Yes. And I kept my end."

The recorder clicked off, the small sound jarring, like the last breath of something that had died long before.

—KEERTHANA NALAMOTHULA (she/her)

NONFICTION

It's winter now, but it was summer then.

One hand planted on either arm of his recliner, Warren stands. He already has on his makeshift coat: a quilted gray and black flannel shirt. Sized extra-large to fit over his belly, its tails hang nearly down to his knees, its sleeves, rolled up to their elbows, dangle near his wrists. He grabs a red bandanna from his pile on the table by the door and ties it around his neck like a necktie. The tails of the knot he ties are shorter than they were forty years ago. He yanks his gray knitted cap from his chest pocket and pulls it onto his head, tugging it over his ears. I stand up from my chair, too, standing still a moment to steady myself.

He walks out of the living room to the kitchen—he rolls now when he walks. I follow him to the kitchen. Warren opens the door to the back porch. He steps down and crosses to the stairs. He picks up the long stick he's cut to use as a cane from where it leans against the railing. I watch him from behind the closed kitchen door. Holding the rail the entire time with both hands, cane hanging between interlocked thumbs, he steps down again, right leg leading the way to each step, three more steps to the back yard. He makes his way, across the ruts of our driveway, to the trail that goes past the greenhouse and the garden.

Warren and his cane disappear where the path curves between peach and apple trees. This means that he'll be working by his barn at the far end of the garden. When the sun gets lower, I'll find him there, scraping wax off old honeycomb, or nailing together a bat house, or maybe sitting nearby, beer in hand, watching the snow melt off his garden, waiting for his winter rye to sprout. I sit back down at our kitchen table and open my laptop.

Yesterday, I read about a man who'd been bitten by a bat but refused treatment, not thinking he needed it. The bat had rabies. The man died.

When I told Warren about it over breakfast this morning, he informed me, gravely: "Bats around here don't bite. That should have told him right off he was in trouble."

I consider how much has changed in the forty years we've lived here, in this tiny, old house with the big yard. Our first winter here, the yard was a moonscape. The previous owners liked yard work even less than I do. Their solution was to cut down all the trees and mow down any other vegetation that might dare emerge. When we arrived in January, a white blanket of snow hid the true state of the yard: brown dirt and mostly brown grass.

Warren fixed all that. He started that spring by laying out most of the yard in garden, tilling half an acre of the sandy soil, fertilizing it well, and planting corn and cabbages, beans and tomatoes, eggplants and watermelons. He built a big greenhouse at the front end of the plot, and a four-room shed at the back end—a little house, really, sided in green, with concrete foundation and floor, an attic and its own lean-to shed on the far side. He planted trees everywhere, fast-growing golden rain trees to break up the bareness right away, and cultivars—redbud, red maple, magnolias, camellias, witch hazel—to greet each spring and summer with successive waves of color and scent.

Even as an old man, Warren is still hardy, but in those days, nobody could match him. Many days, after work, I'd pull into our driveway to find Warren, back from working his bee yards in faraway fields, already in his garden, barefoot, hoeing out weeds, or booted, pushing his big rototiller. Black-bearded, fur-chested, and trim, in those days he favored short, cut-off jeans and blue tank-cut undershirts, if he wore a shirt at all. I'd wave to him from the car and holler. He'd look up and wave back, then pull his red bandanna out of his back pocket and mop his face and chest, before tying it in a pirate band around his forehead. Then he would turn back to keeping his green charges safe.

Now, as then, on hot summer evenings here, bats emerge just after sundown from their roosts, looking to feed on flying insects. A garden in bloom provides a special attraction to bats. They swoop down and scoop up the moths that make a gardener's life hard—coddling, cabbage, cutworm, and squash borer—and any other fliers or hoppers caught out at nightfall. Even swarming mosquitoes, if there are enough of them, can make a meal.

You can hear bats soar above the garden in the dark. Their echoing calls are too high-pitched to hear as notes, but you can detect their cries as clicks, a leisurely *tch-tch-tch* as they glide overhead, seeking prey, then a sudden rush into tick-tick-tick when they spot something tasty and swoop in for the catch. If they come in close enough, you feel wing-beaten air push against your skin as they rush past. Then, successful, they doppler back into their sleepy *tch-tch-tch*.

This winter afternoon, the shadows growing long, I shut down my laptop, collect my own coat and head outside to join Warren, to remind him it's time for dinner. I walk down the soggy path to the back end of our yard. I find him slouched back in his chair by the barn, holding his walking stick upright by his side, like that famous photo of Walt Whitman. Our backyard tabby cat rubs up against his legs, her curled tail quivering. Warren stands, bracing his arms on the chair, and walks over next to me where I stand at the corner of his frosted garden. I step behind him and drape my arms around his shoulders. We look together up into the darkening sky, our cold breath smoking before our faces. No bats fly here on this cold winter evening.

Holding the old man tight, I close my eyes and recall one particular summer night the year we moved here. After supper, Warren returned to his garden to hoe tiny weeds between the rows of winter squash just emerging in their rows. I cleared the dishes and then I joined him out there, watching as he finished up the last furrow. He leaned his hoe against the barn door, and we stood there together, watching the sky darken.

"Damn!" I made a face and swatted at my right arm, where mosquitoes were already landing. I got a couple, but more flew off, only to return to feed again. I swatted again, at both arms, and now at my bare legs, too. "I have to get inside!"

"Wait a minute!" Warren insisted, "Hold still!" Keeping bees, Warren never cared about bugs biting him. I grimaced, but I didn't move.

Then the bats appeared. Tiny flashes of movement at the corner of my eye, they appeared as fleeting as meteors at the beginning of a shower. Then, like meteors, they were everywhere in the glowing sky, darting and weaving way above the newly disturbed dirt. I stood next to Warren for a few moments, hearing metronomic clicks, watching the wonder in the sky.

My legs itched all over. I looked down, to see a horde of mosquitoes feasting on my calves. I yelped, and ran toward the house, slapping at my arms and legs as I ran.

But when I got to the greenhouse, I stopped. I turned back to see Warren standing by the back edge of the garden, looking skyward, lit by dying sunlight. While I watched, he peeled his tank top off over his beard and the bandanna-bound tangle of his hair. Holding his shirt at his side, he stepped forward, to stand barefoot in the dirt. Still looking upward, he spread his arms slightly out from his hips and lifted his sweaty chest, offering himself as sacrifice to the mosquitoes drawn to his end-of-day smell of sweat and dirt and hair and skin. He stood, a garden statue cast in bronze.

Then, all around Warren, in the last light of day, I made out the flash and flurry of bats as they swooped in to feed on the motes that swarmed his sweating body. They found the feast their benefactor provided. They drenched my shining love in sonar. They fanned his skin with soft leather wings.

—DAVID MILLEY (he/him)
First published in Halfway Down the Stairs

I say one thing, my grief says another.

Fortesa Latifi was right. I say it should not be like this. My grief holds me by the throat and says, *but it is like this.*

It is like this.

You, riding the carousel. Short top, a sliver of skin showing, loose waist bead blushing in rainbow colours. Your eyes darkened with liner and a desire to burn yourself and the world. Walking arm in arm with her. It is a pretty dusk—the sun's embers, orange and purple—the colour of magical beginnings and findings. You are smiling in your pictures like everything is okay, like everything is as it should be.

It is like this.

I am once again covered in dirt. I woke up to find myself in yet another grave—the dirt everywhere, even in my mouth. I do not know what day or time it is. I do not know what number of grave this is I have to dig myself out of. The phone plays the song, *I am in the backseat of the cop's car watching the party alive,* living through the house lights and the people. I am always on the outside looking in. I look at your pictures. The ferris wheel shimmering in the background, another party, another connection to the living I am missing out on. I stay still in horror, watching as the carnival of life passes me by.

It is like this.

You do what you want now. All commitment has ever been to you is a chain. Something holding you back from living your best life. Now there is no anchor tying you to the ocean floor. You do not have to be underwater. Even the mermaids barely remember your name. You float in and out of rooms—a lingering memory. Your body movements all anew, intentions cast on your hardened heart. It must be insanely freeing to be able to shed off the weight of another body so easily. To simply say, "I am done. I am moving on now" and for it to be so. To step into another landscape of life— this one that I am not a part of—this one that is more vibrant, more colourful. Forgetting your pain and the one you cause has always been your greatest gift. I underestimated how sharp and deep your forgetting cuts, especially when all I do is remember.

It is like this.

I have to take pills to fall asleep and even those are not enough. I am tied to the ocean floor by memory. I have been underwater for so long I am turning a sad blue like the room he slept in before he died. The water is the only living thing touching me. I visit you and you do not know what to do with your hands. Neither do I. The first time you hug me I crack like glass—it has been so long since I have felt a human body. I know this might be the last.

It should not be like this. You should not be okay. Happy. Smiling. Hopeful. Falling in love with life and your carefree youth, while I struggle to breathe. Lungs full of water. 21 pills arranged in a row. Counting minutes to unconsciousness. It should not be like this.

But it is.

This is grief.

P.S.

I have dug myself out of innumerable graves. I will be damned if I do not say: this is another hole that is not my final grave, I have survived. And it has your name all over it.

—SANTUELLA KIMANI (she/her)

At seventeen years, six months, and six days old, I injected heroin for the first time.

At this point, I was in an abusive relationship with a twenty something year old who got me addicted to the opiates he sold. Anthony was also an addict who had recently made the transition from snorting to shooting up and had been poorly hiding it for weeks. He'd sneak off to the bathroom for ten, fifteen, twenty minutes at a time to run the shower before coming out dry and in the clothes he'd been wearing. Jammed up beyond all recognition.

I'd begun begging for complete honesty between us while promising no punitive relationship measures, but to no avail. I'd question him, and he'd dismiss it. I'd search his things and find needles for him to swear they belonged to his friends. I opened the door on him injecting, and still, he looked me in the face and denied it. Tourniquet tied off with blood dripping down his arm; he swore that I was crazy.

He was that kind of dude. He would never, in a million years, own up to or admit to shit. And he would try out his believability with me when he'd test run lies.

***

Earlier that summer he'd busted in the door, screaming how he'd lost all the money I'd given him to go and cop. Tossing pillows, and flipping couch cushions, throwing the contents of his pockets across the room. Ready to rip his hair out, face red and veins popping out of his forehead and neck. He crumbled into a heaving pile on the floor. I'd started to cry. Withdrawals so bad my bones hurt to stand, I slumped off the chair hopelessly and crawled over to where he was, pounding his fists into the linoleum while panting. I wrapped my arms around his frail body to keep him from hurting himself.

"It's okay. Shh, it's okay." My tears slid around my chin and down my neck, pooling in my bra in sets of twos. Then, as if nothing had happened, he stood up with an emotionless expression. Looking down at me with a blank stare, he pulled, from the small front pocket in his jeans, a gram and tossed it where I was kneeling.

"Wh-what the fuck, Tony?" Wiping the salt-wet streaks from my face and chin, I felt my panic and desperation turn to absolute rage—admittedly with a dreg of relief that I wouldn't be left sick. That's the power he and heroin had over me. As horrible, rotten, sadistic, and cruel as they were, I was always grateful when they showed up, and all transgressions were immediately forgiven. He knew this and took full advantage in every way he could.

He waltzed over and started to straighten the lopsided cushions, fluffing the decorative pillows before he sat down to watch TV. As if nothing had happened. Not saying a word to one another, I anxiously tore into the small plastic bag.

It was a week later that he'd call his dealer and put on a similar performance, saying he was robbed for all his money and drugs after he'd really just gone on a week-long isolated bender, nodding out while playing Call of Duty.

But it was the day I opened his bedroom door while he was injecting that we stopped speaking for weeks. He knew there was no made up story to tell. No excuse, nor denying. He could only rely on gaslighting. *"You are crazy and that is not what you saw."* And while that tactic worked for 99% of our relationship . . . I was not unhinged enough to imagine someone using drugs intravenously. So, he just stopped taking my calls all together.

I couldn't understand it. What had I done wrong? It broke my heart, but I decided maybe it was for the best and I went back to rehab.

*****

What people fail to understand about detox is that it's not unlike prison. That's where we got most ideas for what to do when we are back on the street again. We would swap stories and trade successfully executed plays, quick come-ups, foolproof cash schemes, and share tips on how to get high in practically any scenario or situation. Because I was still a minor in an adolescent facility, it was a disorienting experience seeing the fellow patients and what they were in for. You always had the kids with the highly protective parents who caught them smoking weed in their garage once and sent them off for a 30-day, learn your lesson the hard way, boot camp.

Then there were the kids, like myself, who were in for harder drugs. And inevitably, harder lifestyles. Most had been exposed to serious trauma in the process. There they all were crammed in one room. Some after being sex trafficked and pimped out. Some after contracting incurable diseases. Most of us, after losing everything and everyone. Mixed with teens who just missed their Xbox and beating off in solitude. It was a fucking weird dynamic. But one thing was absolutely, undeniably true; despite the ruthless teasing, the kids who were on the harder side would fucking kill for the kids who weren't.

***

I always arrived late at night for intake. And it was at breakfast the next morning I saw a frail fourteen year old I was sectioned with last time. His name was Gabe. He was so timid and nervous, just looking at him too long he'd start to shake. He really didn't have a drug problem, but the system did not know what to do with this poor kid. He had bounced all over Massachusetts foster homes, and in between he'd serve time in different respites and hospitals. He'd attempted suicide four times that they knew of on record, and the last two were by pills. So the state had him sent to rehab to learn about the dangers of drugs before sending him to his new home—wherever it would be. He was a good kid, and my heart hurt for him.

As soon as he noticed me, he raised his trembling hand hesitantly to wave at me and gave a half smile. I winked at him waiting in line for my meal; a cup of "welcome back, don't tell the other kids", hot decaf coffee. Just then, some chunky dweeb just brought in from Brockton's juvenile hall came up and snatched his fruit cup and his cereal while talking shit about how he didn't need it after filling up on snacks from under the sink. I rolled my eyes and grabbed a tray. I really did not want to go into confinement my first day, and fuck, if only I didn't want that coffee . . . but here we go. Yet, it was just as I turned that I saw this beast of a man, wearing inpatient scrubs, stand up from the back corner and tower over everyone at six and a half feet. He took two steps and latched his hands around this fat kid's neck and slammed him into the ground. Gabe's fruit cup smashed all over the floor, and for the first time in my life I actually heard the wind being knocked out of someone's chest. I quietly slid the tray back and waited for the recovery specialists and guards to break it up.

At least I knew where my table was.

***

A few days later, I learned his name was Pete. He was from Middleboro, he was an IV user, and he had a clinically insane older brother. Somehow

202

that was all I needed to know. When are we gonna hang out and get high outside of here? He would turn 18 during his thirty days, and naturally, the second he did, he signed himself out. On a stack of Post-It's I'd swiped from my clinician's office, I tallied the days off until I could make a break for it myself. I think somewhere deep down I knew what was going to happen before it did. I don't know when or where along the way, but I had already blindly agreed to follow Anthony down this path. Wherever it would take us. Wherever it would take me back to him.

***

Pete hopped the turnstile and boarded the commuter rail to come and meet me the day I was released.

"Did you bring everything?" For the first time, I felt myself shake like Gabe.

He nodded slowly, solemnly.

Watching my veins rise while he slapped my arm, I decided to look away like I would at the doctor's office. Focus on something else; my eyes darted around the room seeking a distraction. I'd heard him flick the syringe. Find something, anything else.

The peel away Post-It's calendar I'd made.

It's November 11th.

I winced at the pinch, and before I could exhale . . . I felt it.

No longer scared, or any emotion, I looked back at my extended arm while he finished.

I read the words on the side of the needle as an omen for what was to come.

Use Once And Destroy

—AMANDA IZZO (she/her)

When was the last time you heard a Native American perspective—on anything? Politics? Music? Education? You probably haven't. And that's a shame. In a way, it's the inverse of how Black Americans are often handled in the media—constantly spotlighted, highlighted, and gaslighted. We are visible, but not always *seen*.

The Choctaw and Scleroderma

So you can imagine my shock when, in researching scleroderma—a rare autoimmune disease that hardens the skin and connective tissue—I repeatedly came across one Native group I had never heard much about: the Choctaw. I was familiar with the Cherokees, the Sioux, the Chippewa, and the Seminoles. But the Choctaw? Not at all.

A rheumatologist told me that members of the Choctaw Nation of Oklahoma are three times more likely to develop scleroderma than the general population.

"Why?" I asked.

"No one knows for sure," was the answer.

It reminded me of the long-documented devastation that smallpox and yellow fever wrought upon Indigenous communities—disasters introduced by colonial contact. Could it be a hereditary virus? Genetic testing for scleroderma offers few answers. The disease is rare, even among the populations in which it's more prevalent. Most Choctaw people don't have it—just as most individuals of African or Mediterranean descent don't develop sickle cell disease, and Tay-Sachs is rare even among Ashkenazi Jews, though many carry the gene.

The Elusive Nature of Knowledge

When illness strikes, we're often told knowledge is power. But in this case, knowledge is elusive. There is little information on scleroderma. Its exact causes are unknown. Like many autoimmune diseases, it seems to stem from immune system dysfunction, but that's where the certainty ends.

The Legacy of Native Ancestry in the Black Community

In the Black community, stories of Native ancestry are common. Many of us were raised with tales of grandmothers who had long, straight black hair, high cheekbones, or a reddish tint to their skin. These were often the only tangible links we had to Indigenous heritage. And yet, we seldom pursue these claims further.

As Zora Neale Hurston once quipped, "I am the only Negro in the United States whose grandfather on the mother's side was not an Indian chief." She was poking fun at the prevalence of these oral histories, but also underscoring how often our roots are based more on myth than documentation.

Tracing Roots and the African American Experience

I've never traced my ancestry. I assume—like many African Americans—that my ancestors were kidnapped and forced onto slave ships. Somewhere during that dehumanizing transatlantic voyage, they ceased to be seen as human. This loss of identity is central to America's evolution: it is, for better or worse, a country built on the shifting sands of imposed and inherited identity.

Historian Tiya Miles and others have noted that there were indeed ports and plantations that connected Indigenous and African communities. Some Black families recall oral histories about enslaved ancestors escaping and finding refuge with Native nations. Though it did happen, historians like Malinda Maynor Lowery and others caution that such occurrences were relatively rare.

The Intersection of Black and Native American Histories

Genetically, Native Americans are most closely related to East Asians and Ancient North Eurasians. Their DNA carries signals from Western

Eurasia, traced back to a shared Siberian population during the Upper Paleolithic era. And of course, every human alive today ultimately descends from Africa.

Despite the mythology we're often fed about purity of bloodlines, the reality is far more complicated. For example, studies suggest that the average African American has at least 12.5 percent European ancestry—more often than Native American. Actor Don Cheadle, in the PBS series *African American Lives*, discovered his ancestors were enslaved by the Chickasaw Nation. That revelation, while historically accurate, can be emotionally jarring. It challenges the romanticized notion that Native Americans and Black people shared unbroken solidarity.

The Choctaw, Slavery, and the 'Civilized Tribes'

The Choctaw were one of the so-called Five Civilized Tribes, along with the Cherokee, Creek, Chickasaw, and Seminole. These tribes adopted European-style agriculture and, at the urging of the federal government, also adopted the practice of slavery. The aim was to "civilize" them in the eyes of white Americans, but at the cost of complicity in the same systems of oppression that had once targeted them.

The Environmental Dilemma

It was around then that I stopped digging. I fell into the rabbit hole of "bad blood" and blood quantum—the controversial system the U.S. government uses to determine Native American heritage. It struck me: here I was, trying to trace disease through history, and all I kept finding were the politics of identity.

Would environmental exposure be a better explanation? Possibly. But even if I uncovered a trigger, I couldn't un-breathe the air. I couldn't un-expose myself. And that's when I kept encountering the word: silica.

Silica and Its Hidden Dangers

Silica is a mineral found in sand, granite, glass. It's everywhere. But when inhaled in its microscopic form—as dust—it becomes toxic. It can damage the lungs and immune system, potentially triggering autoimmune responses like scleroderma.

Did I inhale it?

These particles are invisible, ever-present, and impossible to track.

How, in the hell, should I know?

—ALLISON WHITTENBERG (she/her)

When I was young, my older sister raised nine minnows that she had caught from a stream. Because I was so young, I don't remember which stream we caught them from or what the fish tank where the minnows lived looked like, but I do remember that the minnows kept dying. It is common for fish to jump out of the water surface and die, but seeing them die with their noses stuck in sand or eating each other was quite a shock to me as a preschooler.

I remember changing the tank water while sitting on a small, red plastic chair in the bathroom with my mom and sister: we took the fish out of the tank, put them in a red basin, and put them back into the tank when it was over. The three of us never got used to this difficult task. We thoroughly washed the sand grains and the decorations we had put inside them, rubbing them with our hands. The sand grains would be covered with excrement from the nine minnows and puffed-up fish food, giving off a strange, fishy smell. My mom also scrubbed and cleaned with her fingers each leaf of tiny fake aquatic plants that we had planted.

The fish was dead with its nose stuck between the aquatic plants and the sand that had been so diligently cleaned. Its facial expression was very creepy. As I think of it now, we didn't even remove the toxins from the tap water, didn't consider the temperature or oxygen concentration of the water, and changed the water way too frequently. Maybe that's why the fish always looked sick. It was natural that they had to jump out of the water for oxygen. When my older sister saw the protruding corpse of a minnow, she cried out of fear and left it to my dad to throw it away in the toilet. I thought she was being such a drama queen. Until Pink, the second pink fish I raised, died the same way.

If you go somewhere like Walmart, there are always fish in the pet section. I know that sometimes the fish are put in a plastic bag and given out for free. (To digress for a moment, I think distributing fish in plastic bags is the same as painting chicks with lacquer and selling them at 500 won each.)

While passing by, I saw a light pink goldfish and fell in love with it at first sight. Mom seemed to like it too; so she opened her wallet and offered to buy it for me. She also asked me about the silver-blue fish next to it, saying that a fish would get lonely if it stayed alone. Thus, carrying two fish and gravel to put at the bottom of a fish tank, determined to keep these fish for a long time, I went home, checking on the way if the fish got motion sick in the shaking car. When I got home, my mom brought out a little square transparent glass vase—I could not tell where she had found it—and suggested that we raise the fish in it. Again, it was too small to raise the two fish in it, but at that time, I thought it was perfect. I named the pink fish Pink King and the silver-blue fish Bitna (its meaning "shiny") King, so that they would live long and grow big. My sister said the names were ugly, but I believed that animals raised with ugly names would live longer.

A classmate of mine raised a goldfish for three years. She said that she often forgot to change the water and would change it when she noticed it had turned yellowish green. She sometimes forgot to feed the fish too. So I decided to change the water less frequently than last time. Pink King and Bitna King certainly lived longer than the minnows, but the fish's expressions began to darken when Bitna's fins were injured and its sides turned red. The wound looked like it had been caused by my mother's fingernails when she had caught it trying to escape and get into the food hole. Fish are so fragile. Bitna got torn so easily without any effort at all and died after suffering in pain.

As my mother said, Pink must have felt lonely, staying alone. The tank was near the front door. I checked the condition of Pink every time I left home or came back, but one morning, there was nothing in the fish tank. I panicked a bit and checked the bottom of the shoe area. Half of Pink was there, crushed, and she was still wet. Probably, it was I who stepped on her. Just like my sister had done, I dragged my mom out of the kitchen and showed her Pink. Mom took out a piece of tissue, wrapped her up, and flushed her down the toilet, just like my dad had done with the minnows. The last look at Pink made me go through a hard time. The image of my dad flushing each of the minnows down the toilet overlapped with the image of him releasing the last surviving minnows back into the stream; I thought, it might have been better to release Pink into the stream when Bitna died. But humans have endless greed and repeat the same mistakes, right?

I received four guppies when I bought flowerpots from the flower shop below the art academy: a carnation pot for Parents' Day and a small empty pot. The flower shop lady told me that the small pot would produce oxygen on its own. She asked me if I wanted to put it in a fish tank and gave me the baby guppies, smaller than a fingernail. Her fish tanks were hidden here and there among the pots of the forest-like flower shop. The guppies there were big and chubby, and some of them even boasted colorful tails.

They must have eaten a lot and grown fat to become as big as fingers. If I raised the small guppies for a long time, they would become gorgeous, the lady said.

I received the four guppies in a paper cup and blocked the top of the cup with my palm to avoid spilling it in my dad's car. When I got home, I looked back at the fish tank where Pink and Bitna had lived. This time, I laid down no sand or gravel. Now that I had a high schooler's brain, I guess I never wanted to see a fish die with its nose in the bottom again. Placing the small pot said to automatically generate oxygen on the glass bottom, I told myself that this would become a playground for the guppies. I would inject oxygen to the fish tank using a dropper and add the tap water to the tank only after removing toxins from it. I changed the water only when I thought that too much poop had accumulated in the tank, putting the fish in a cup I had used when brushing my teeth. Seeing me doing all that, my dad told me to raise them well this time and get some fine gravel and high-quality fish food somewhere. I thought it would be nice to have pebbles at the bottom of the fish tank.

The guppies were small. They were too small, and they swam fast, accordingly. As the top of the fish tank was too narrow, I had to figure out a way to scoop them up when changing the water. I would drop food on the surface, and when they came up to eat it, I caught them with a bottle cap. With that cap, two guppies were squashed. They were swimming close to the wall of the tank, driven away by the current I created while carefully trying to scoop them up. I believe I was being overconfident since the guppies at that time had grown up to reach the size of a thumbnail from that of a pinky nail.

When adding water to the bare glass bottom, it was okay to pour it in right away. After laying the gravel underneath, I had to carefully let it flow down along the wall. Otherwise, its pressure could make pebbles shake and end up injuring the guppies' heads.

One day, I saw a guppy floating on the water. He had been swimming in one corner for a while after being hit by the pebbles. It felt so strange that he would stay floating in one corner and looking blank. I turned the fish tank around, but the guppy swam back to where it had been. Then he ended his life.

The last guppy jumped out and disappeared. Now I could send the dead guppies down the toilet myself because I had grown up.

I felt quite melancholic. No matter how small a being was, death was death, and I was the one to blame for it. And speaking of a toilet, is this the way to mourn death? Back then, I thought there was nothing I could do about it; however, I could have at least cared enough to let them be buried under the flower bed in front of my apartment.

I haven't raised anything since then. Not only do I have no confidence in keeping them for long, but I also remember the faces of the fish. Of course, I remember every single animal I raised. I remember turtles and frogs, and I can even recall what flowers I grew. In addition, I know that if I let something go, it will be unbearably sad. Later, when I become capable enough to create the best environment for whatever I will raise, I will take responsibility for it. In remembrance of the fifteen fish that were sent away . . .

—Okbi Han (she/her)

BALLS

Zola Craft Gallery was a magical place. It was the kind of place you went to buy a gift for someone else. Each item was not just made, but crafted. The mirrors at Zola Craft Gallery reflected a person more beautiful than one expected. Each frame promised to hold memories that you had yet to imagine. Each tiny trinket is a chance to feel lovely, to be lovely. The charming bags, designed to hold bottles of wine. Shining balls to fill bowls, just for decoration.

Alone at my post at Zola Craft Gallery, a little retail space tucked above the bagel shop on Ninth St, I did feel the slightest of tremor when he appeared at the top of the stairwell leading into our open shop. As I observed him, I had no idea that he also observed me—young (only 22), solitary, back to the window—nowhere to run or hide.

I had observed this figure around Durham, his bulky form moving ungainly through the Perkins Library Reference Area, soft hands reaching for the door knob leading up to the mostly empty stacks.

I had observed this person because something about him said "Not a Duke Student." The absurd bowl haircut? Lips, a bit too red? Ill-fitting shirts, taut against the drum of a tummy?

Later, I hated myself for being so naïve, so vulnerable, so available. So curious, also. What was he doing with his back towards me for so long?

I must have been looking down, away for a moment. At some merchandise? The register? A clandestine novel I tucked under the counter at quiet moments like this one?

Something in the room shifted. His breath? The timbre of the air conditioning? The traffic outside?

I looked up, and there he was, making direct eye contact. There it was. I saw him fondling his wrinkly ball sack.

I saw the shop's glass shelving, ready to splinter into shards. I saw silver jewelry in the counter showcase, glinting like kitchen knives. I saw picture frames, the edges at dangerous angles. I saw ghoulish lawn figurines, ready to maim. I saw weighty pottery mugs, glazed in lead.

A voice I didn't recognize said, "Get out of here. I'm calling the police." The voice is mine.

I didn't see him leave the shop, but I sprinted down the stairwell to lock the front door, to momentarily turn our sign to Closed as I waited for the police officers to come, to tell me there's nothing they can do. Police officers who will tell me to stop calling 911, even though the man will call the store repeatedly, just to promise me "I'm going to hump your heinie." I told the police officers that I am alone in this store, that I live alone, that I've seen this person before.

Again they told me, there's nothing they can do.

And there's nothing that I can do either, except turn the sign back to Open, to wipe my sweaty fingerprints from the shining glass door, open to the public. Nothing I can do but return to my station, to straighten the trinkets, the frames, the balls, the bags.

—RACHEL LUTWICK-DEANER (she/her)

Expanding outwards and inwards at the same time.

I am reading something C. wrote, and it is so clean and sterile in how it cuts my heart. But also so comforting in how the shape of this knife, the sharp of this blade is familiar, that someone else knows a little bit of what it feels like to feel like this.

It makes me want to share a little more of my heart, of my innate joy and quiet deep sorrow. It's like she said, hearing someone bare their heart is a signal of safety, a beacon of belonging if not of hope or comfort.

The tarot reader, one of my favourites, said this month is for belonging. Soon after, I am reeling with the Otherness that perennially stalks me. Surprisingly and joyfully, I am moving a little past the edges into the land of belonging. Yet sometimes, I find myself frozen in the division between me and the people I am with. Moments of sudden stillness, where I am more of an observer, less of a participant, more of an idea, less of a human. It is clinically satisfying in how much it hurts, how much it guts me, to see the same pattern unfold.

The boy in the book, a stark bearer of all my desperate, insecure parts, said his sham is pitiful. Not his otherness. Not his shame. Not his identity. Not even himself. But his trials at being more, at being seen, really seen, at being connected, at belonging; those are pitiful, because they are a failing he can't stop. One he can't help. I sat on the bed and cried. My sham is pitiful isn't it? I will not look in the mirror to see where the cracks are. I will wear the pretty dress, spin around in circles and be one with the wind. Saying *I am not one for staying in one place too long,* saying *this careless flow is my true nature.* saying *I do not prefer rootedness.* I will pretend. Even if it's for the night and day. And the whole week after as we work together.

Then I will sit on my bed at night. And cry because the sham is pitiful. Where is true belonging in this world?

I have found parts of it in unlikely places, people I have never met, lives I have never lived. It has been fine. Except I deeply desire those places and lives to bleed into this one I am in currently. Swallowing it whole as if there were no absence previously. I am trying to belong and I now recognize belonging as a spiral—you keep returning to certain moments, only from a different point in time, from another layered version of your being.

I am sitting face to face with a sad truth—a part of me thinks I am not truly enough as I am, thinks I have to be some way, some person, thinks it would be easier to belong then. I think to myself how much I have made this place a safe home, only to find I am still playing kaleidoscope; still putting up a certain front for a certain gaze. It all comes crashing down.

What a mess! What a sham!—it would be pitiful were it not for its heartbreaking principle. I am trying again and again, to spiral outwards and inwards at the same time. Learning, trying, crying my way towards belonging with myself in the present moment. Knowing I will be back here and I would love to have had more grace and love for this version of me.

I said let's be ourselves.

This is the time.

I will wear the pretty dress and stay. Saying *thanks for inviting me. I am glad to be here.*

—SANTUELLA KIMANI (she/her)

i have been carving into my brain like clay
clumsily
the grit of my past derailing me as my hands try to trace new grooves for
    my thoughts to flow into
jagged, shallow grooves because i don't want to break the delicate slab i
    have so preciously pinched into just the right shape.

dan leaving did something to me.

after years of interrupting my violent wildcat survival machine with his
soft, kind acceptance—a type of love i had never felt before, that makes
me wonder if i'd ever felt someone's love at all—he left me. so completely,
decidedly, unbudgingly.

he left me with such finality that after he walked out i never saw him again.
i never spoke to him again. i never received his soft, kind acceptance again.
i spent grueling winter days dying in our apartment in jamaica plain. i
thought i would never get out of bed again. i called my mother, sobbing so
viscerally my wails went silent and my air ran out the way it used to when
i was a baby and my mother was overwhelmed by the fussy firstborn that
had sent her into such a postpartum depression she could not even hold
me while i cried so breathless, silent and red-faced that all the other
women in the house passed me around until my grandmother came to
toss me in the air and with the shock suspend my toil. i called this mother
because she's the only one i have. i had no one else to call. who else had
seen me wailing, silent, red-faced and still offered me love? it had
sometimes been her, eventually, in my young adulthood. and it had always
been dan, consistently, in my late 20s.

consistently. his warmth was something i could expect. his big arms
around me, my cheek on his meaty chest, my soft belly meshing with his,
his body around mine, marsupial. the things i expected. my body still
remembers what it felt like to breathe inside those arms. to breathe love.
stillness. it may have been the first arms that held me breathing. my lungs
truly filling, my heart rate slowing, my world building.

when i scrape lines into this slab of clay i am trying to make it into a leaf,
carving its veins. first i scrape along the middle, wanting to curve softly and
instead leaving an insecure, pointed scratch along the length of my piece.
i'm not satisfied, but i keep going. there's nothing i can do to fix the past.

the rest of the lines make me feel desperate. they're facing the wrong direction, they're jagged as they try to make smooth curves, they're cutting too deep into this 1/8-inch sheet that's dry and brittle and might break if i exhale in the wrong moment. i start to feel inexplicable tears building behind my eyes. don't talk to me right now, or i'll cry.

this is what it's like to heal your brain from trauma. i don't know what it looks like but it's what everybody tells me i am doing. they've said my brain has roads inside its forest, ways it knows to get from here to there, to take a stimulus from where it arrives toward the place my brain knows how to interpret it. if A, then B. if this, then that. if start of the road, then end of the road. and i am trying to build new ones.

because the old ones told me if my mother loved me, she would ignore me. push me away, avoid me, not want to touch me. this is what love felt like.

and if my father loved me he would berate me. scream at me, hit me, leave home because of me and later hug me, no apology. this is what love felt like.

if love, then pain.

i keep carving

—CAROLINA MURRIEL (she/they)

ABOUT THE CONTRIBUTORS

✳ **Alex Carrigan** (he/him) is a Pushcart-nominated editor, poet, and critic from Alexandria, VA. He is the author of *Now Let's Get Brunch* (Querencia Press, 2023) and *May All Our Pain Be Champagne* (Alien Buddha Press, 2022). He has appeared in *SoFloPoJo, Cotton Xenomorph, Bullshit Lit, HAD, fifth wheel press*, and more. Visit carriganak.wordpress.com or follow him on Twitter @carriganak for more info.

✳ **Alexei Raymond** (he/him) chases visions of unspeakable loveliness from a world lost. He is an ardent fan of rabbits, insects, and monkeys. Born in the Middle East, he is currently based in Belgrade. His stories appear in publications such as *Blood+Honey, The Crawfish*, and *Everscribe Magazine.* Connect with him at https://x.com/enemyofcruelty

✳ **Alexis Barton** (she/her) is a poet and student from Woodstock, GA. Her work can be found in *Sheepshead Review, The Journal of Undiscovered Poets, The Listening Eye*, and more, and her debut poetry collection is set to be published by *Dipity Press* by the end of 2025. She works as a poetry reader for *Chestnut Review* and attends Kennesaw State University to become an editor. In her spare time, she enjoys baking macarons, drinking coffee, and watching the rain. Insta: @alexisinink

✳ **Allison Whittenberg** is an award winning novelist and playwright. Her poetry has appeared in *Columbia Review, Feminist Studies, J Journal*, and *New Orleans Review*. Whittenberg is an eight-time Pushcart Prize nominee. *They Were Horrible Cooks* is her collection of poetry.

✳ **Amanda Izzo** (she/her) is a writer and artist from Boston, MA. Though published in other mediums, she has enjoyed the art of creative writing for over a decade. This year, she has begun to share comprehensive and detailed recollections of her life and youth in the form of nonfiction narratives. Her newest pieces titled, "Tell Me Where it Hurts" and "Consent Defined" were published by Levitate Magazine in May 2025.

✳ **Angel Sylvia** is a writer and an artist, creating in Dharug Sydney. She is the creator behind local Sydney publications, *The Dream Zine* and *SMEER Mag*.

✳ **Ann Grogan** is a joyful octogenarian, retired lawyer, and emerging writer and poet who lives in San Francisco, CA. Her writing promotes the unequivocal permission to pursue one's passions at any age. Her poems have appeared in *Little Old Lady,* the University of Vermont's *Continuing Education Newsletter*, and KAWL Public Media "Bay Poets", and her poems are forthcoming in the fall editions of *The Prairie Review* and *Amethyst Review*. She's the author of two volumes of poetry, *Poetic Musings on Pianos, Music & Life* and invites readers to visit her music & poetry website, rhapsodydmb.com.

✳ **Augustina Naanret Dasat** (she/her) is an emerging poet whose writing is shaped by introspection, observation, and an engagement with the inner workings of the mind. Rooted in both the personal and the philosophical, she writes to explore the edges of thought and emotion, to make sense of the complexities of being. She is currently based in Abuja, Nigeria and has performed poetry at local arts and theater shows. When not herding cattle in the morning, fishing in the afternoons, or critiquing in the evening,

✳ **Bryce Mauzy** is usually watching the tube with a pen and paper in hand. He is a Navy burnout that since has received an education and now works as a non-profit educator for the incarcerated.

✳ **Carolina Murriel** (she/they) is an artist, journalist and death doula in Louisiana. She makes essays, poetry and ceramic sculpture about immigration and mental illness. Carolina is a Tin House Summer Workshop and Macondo Writers Workshop scholar, and her work is in NPR.org, *Audible, California Sunday Magazine,* the Undocupoets anthology *Here to Stay,* and more. She cofounded *Pizza Shark,* a podcast studio working toward radical inclusivity in media. They've won Webbys, iHeartRadio Podcast Awards, and more.

✳ Brutal honesty, humor, a quirky imagination, & a wide range of topics all feature in **Christine Fowler's** poems. She aims to make them accessible & sometimes to challenge or surprise. The common thread through all her experience has been working with people at a point of change in their life often involving a traumatic transition in very challenging circumstances. It is this lifetime of experience that she now brings to her writing and performance. She has been published in the UK, USA, & Australia.

✳ **Connor Fisher** is the author of *A Renaissance with Eyelids* (Schism Press, 2024), *The Isotope of I* (Schism Press, 2021) and three poetry and hybrid chapbooks including *The Unholy Moon* (salò press, 2024). He has an MFA from the University of Colorado at Boulder and a Ph.D. in Creative Writing and English from the University of Georgia. His writing has appeared in journals including *Denver Quarterly, Random Sample Review, Tammy,* and *Clade Song.* He lives and teaches in north Mississippi.

✳ **Dara Laine** (she/her) is a poet and member of the LGBTQ+ and disabled communities based in Baltimore, originally from a hay farm in New Jersey. She returned to poetry after the sudden death of her father. Her work explores memory, grief, and the sacred ordinary through restrained lyricism and symbolic realism. Her work has appeared in *Right Hand Pointing* and is forthcoming in *American Poetry Journal* and *Pine Hills Review.*

✳ **David Milley's** (he/him/his) work appears in *3rd Wednesday, RFD Magazine, Friends Journal, Bay Windows,* and *The Amphibian.* David lives in southern New Jersey with his husband and partner of forty-nine years, Warren Davy, who's made his living as a farmer, woodcutter, nurseryman, auctioneer, beekeeper, and cook. These days, Warren tends his garden and keeps honeybees. David walks and writes.

✳ **Derek Yen** (he/him) writes code in the mornings and everything else in the evenings. His writing keeps returning to systems of power, chronic illness, and speculative imagination. His poems have been published or are forthcoming in *ANMLY, Seventh Wave, Lucky Jefferson, A Velvet Giant, No, Dear,* and elsewhere. He shares an apartment in Brooklyn with his partner, their dog, and several houseplants. Find him online at speculativeloaf.wordpress.com or on Instagram @derekiswriting.

✳ **Devon Webb** (she/her) is an autistic writer & editor based in Aotearoa New Zealand. Her award-winning work has been published extensively worldwide & accumulated seven Best of the Net/Pushcart nominations. She is currently working on her debut novel & full-length poetry collection & can be found on social media at @devonwebbnz.

✳ **Dylan Night** is a former medical professional and published author most recently in print through *Able Muse, Wingless Dreamer, In Parentheses,* and *Neon Origami.* He resides in San

Diego, California with his partner and stepchild. He is currently workshopping his most recent novel.

* **Emiliano Gomez** (he) has recent work in *Action, Spectacle, Yalobusha, Alchemy, mercuryfirs, Interpret Magazine,* and is a contributor at the *Cleveland Review of Books.* He holds a BA from UCLA and an MFA from Notre Dame.

* **Hailie Cochran** (she/her/hers) is a poet from Macon, Georgia and current MFA candidate at UNC Greensboro. She earned her bachelor's in English and creative writing from Mercer University in 2023. Her work appears both online and in print.

* **Irina Vérène** is a non-binary writer from Germany who loves to explore the rawness and complexity of human connection and emotion in both poetry and prose. Since 2025, they're a staff member of *Sepulchre Literary, Violet Desires, Etherae Magazine, Elora Vérité Magazine, Vermillion Literary,* and *Mildew Zine.* Find them on Instagram (@queen_of_gore) or Substack (@queenofgore).

* **Isabel Lemus Kristensen** (they/them/elle) is a queer, Xicanx multidisciplinary artist and writer living in Portland, Oregon, with their two adorable dogs. Their work has appeared in Portland Monthly, zines + things, and elsewhere.

* **Jonathan Fletcher** holds a Master of Fine Arts in Creative Writing from Columbia University School of the Arts. A Pushcart Prize, Best of the Net, and Best Microfiction nominee, he won Northwestern University Press's Drinking Gourd Chapbook Poetry Prize contest in 2023, for which his debut chapbook, *This is My Body,* was published in 2025. Currently, he serves as a Zoeglossia Fellow and lives in San Antonio, Texas.

* **Josie Yaconelli** (she/her) is a writer, musician, and conceptual artist based in San Francisco, CA. Her work explores gender, queerness, longing, and the many mundane details of being alive. She is an active member, lecturer, and archivist with S.O.S.Q.O.S (the Southern Oregon Society for the preservation of the Queer, Occult, and Strange) and plays mandolin as part of the Front Porch Players, a radical faerie folk band based in Ukiah, CA.

* **Judy Darley** (she/her) is the author of 'The Stairs are a Snowcapped Mountain', 'Sky Light Rain' and 'Remember Me to the Bees'. Her words have been shared aboard boats, in museums and on BBC Radio. She occasionally infiltrates poetry open mic nights with micro stories. Judy lives on England's North Somerset Coast where this story is set. She is currently working on a weird hybrid memoir beast she's not sure how to describe succinctly. Find Judy at @judydarley.bsky.social

* **Julietta Bekker** (she/they) is a writer, Spanish language educator and illustrator who lives with her family in Portland, Oregon. Her poetry is informed by parenting, the natural world, and collective experiences of our socio-political climate. Bekker's illustrations and writing appeared in the newsletter, *Lessons of Survival,* published by The Immigrant Story. Her poetry has been published by *Pile Press, Bitter Melon Review, 7th-Circle Pyrite* and *Seedlings,* with additional pieces forthcoming from *Gather, Flat Ink Magazine* and *Oyster River Pages.* She is currently working on a poetry collection.

* **Justin Hollis** has an MFA in Creative Writing from Hofstra University and currently teaches English and Literature full-time at Palm Beach State College. He lives and writes in Lake Worth, Fl; and his main interest is in the surrealist prose poem.

* **Kai Grenham** (he/him) is an emerging writer based in Virginia. His work has appeared in *New Words Press, WILDSound Writing Festival*, and *Owl Hollow Press*. He adores all things autumnal and magical.

* **Katelyn Stump** is an undergraduate student at Indiana University studying International Law and Institutions who writes poetry in as much free time as she can find. She found her love for poetry through her education, and she aspires to pursue a career in law while maintaining her passion for writing. She finds herself drawn to writing autobiographical pieces that explore her connections with the earth, mental health, relationships, nostalgia, and everything else that swirls in her mind!

* **Keerthana Nalamothula** (She/Her) writes psychological stories that explore complex themes through a subtle, character-driven lens. Favouring tension over spectacle, their work focuses on the undercurrents of power, perception, and moral ambiguity. When not writing, they enjoy dissecting human behaviour and finding inspiration in quiet moments that say more than words.

* **Kianna Amaya** (she/her) is a graduate student and writer from rural North Carolina. A lifelong reader, she loves to explore the world through literature. Her work explores young adulthood, Black Southern life, and the overlooked moments in life through essays and short stories.

* **Konrad Ehresman** (he/him) is a poet and creative living in Northwest Arkansas where he is earning his MFA in poetry. Konrad's work has been featured by: *The Racket, Invisible City, Barbar, The Bluebird Word,* and *Litbreak* among others. His debut chapbook "Something Like Love" is available from *Bottlecap Press*. Konrad's favorite hobbies include baking bread and being a general nuisance. The stealthy are invited to follow Konrad in person, everyone else can find him on Instagram @ProandKon

* **Linda M. Crate** (she/her) is a Pennsylvanian writer whose poetry, short stories, articles, and reviews have been published in a myriad of magazines both online and in print. She has thirteen published chapbooks the latest being: faerie witch queen (fae corps press, April 2025).

* **LW Platt** is a writer from the Midwest who now lives in New York. He has published work in both Fiction and CNF. He is currently an associate editor for *Wallstrait Literary Journal*.

* **Lynne Dolle** is a retired graduate school professor of Curriculum and Instruction and holds a M.S.Ed in Literacy. She taught the craft of writing poetry to both adults and children in the NYCDOE. In 2001, she was the publisher of "Celebrating Student Writing: Creating a Context for Parent Partnerships."

* **May Garner** (She/Her) is a poet and author based out of Dayton, Ohio. She has been crafting and sharing her work online for over a decade now. She is the author of two poetry collections, "Withered Rising" and "Melancholic Muse." Her work has been featured by *Cozy Ink Press, Dreams in Hiding, Querencia Press*, and most recently, *The Ohio Bards Poetry Anthology*. You can find more of her work on Instagram (@crimson.hands).

* **Mel Mancheno** is a human being, an honors psychology student at Middlesex College, a Princeton Transfer Scholar, a National Network for Youth Council Member, and maybe something else.

✷ **Mia Soto | M.S. Blues** is one of the most decorated figures in the literary magazine community. She currently serves on a few magazine boards and has over 270 publications. She's the Editor-in-Chief of *DICED Online* and the Founder & Editor-in-Chief of *The Infinite Blues Review*. In addition to her many literary endeavors, she is a college student and a proud employee in the Mental Health field. She currently resides in the Bay Area, California. Her debut book, *Collected Works: Poetry & Short Stories* can be purchased online through Amazon, Barnes & Noble, and other booksellers—as well as in store at Caspian Books located in Tracy, California.

✷ **Miro** is a writer based in NYC. Her poetry has previously been published in MEARI, Existe Magazine, and Bullshit Lit among others. She is a contributing writer with Voice Noted Music Blog under her government name Mireille Crocco. When Miro isn't putting words on the page, you can find her lost in a book. You can connect with Miro on Instagram @mireille.c.cro

✷ **MW Bewick** grew up in West Cumbria, England. He is co-founder and editor at Dunlin Press. He has been a gardener and a musician, and these days works as a journalist and editor. He always wears black. Work includes *Scarecrow* (2017), *Pomes Flixus* (2020), *The Zircon Ferries* (2021), *The End of Music* (2022) and *A Study of a Long-Lived Magma Ocean on a Young Moon* (2023).

✷ **Naudia Reeves** (she/her) is a queer poet with an MFA from Florida Atlantic University. Born in Florida and now living in Michigan, her work explores queerness, loss, and self-critique—often with a cameo from one of her four mischievous cats. Her poems appear in *The Passionfruit Review, Progenitor, LETTERS Journal* and more.

✷ **Noah Berlatsky** (he/him) is a freelance writer in Chicago. His full-length collections are *Not Akhmatova* (Ben Yehuda Press, 2024), *Gnarly Thumbs* (Anxiety Press, 2025), *Meaning Is Embarrassing* (Ranger, 2025) and *Brevity* (Nun Prophet, 2025).

✷ **Okbi Han** is a poet, painter, and video editor. Her works were published by *SoFloPoJo, Buffalo 8, Biscuit Hill, Bombay Gin, The Gently Mad* and *The Call Center Collective.* Her other work is scheduled to be published on 50 Give or Take.

✷ **Patrick T. Reardon**, a *Chicago Tribune* reporter from 1976 to 2009, is the author of seven poetry collections. His latest is *Every Marred Thing: A Time in America*, the winner of the 2024 Faulkner-Wisdom Prize from the Pirate's Alley Faulkner Society of New Orleans (Lavender Ink). He is a five-time nominee in poetry for a Pushcart Prize. His poetry has appeared in *America, RHINO, Commonweal, After Hours, Autumn Sky, Burningword Literary Journal, Poetry East*, and other journals.

✷ **Rachel Lutwick-Deaner** (she/her) enjoys a bookish life. She has earned degrees from Colgate University, North Carolina State University, and Queens University of Charlotte. She currently teaches writing and literature at Grand Rapids Community College. Rachel's recent publications can be found at *Chaotic Merge, Door=Jar,* and *Story Sanctum.* Her book reviews can be found at *Southern Review of Books* and on Instagram @professor.ld.

✷ **Rais Tuluka** is a writer and public health strategist based in Sacramento. His poetry and essays explore grief, masculinity, and spiritual resilience, and have appeared in *Parentheses Journal* and *Agape Review.* He is the author of *Iron Wrapped in Wool*, a hybrid collection of poems and meditations on identity and inner discipline.

* **Raquel Dionísio Abrantes** (she/her) is a Portuguese poet. She has a Bachelor's Degree and a Master's Degree in Cinema from Universidade da Beira Interior. Raquel gave a Master Class in Writing of Scripts about Narrative Structure. Her writing has been published by literary journals and magazines.

* **Ricardo Nazario y Colón, Ed.D.** is the author of *The Moor of the Bronx* and *Of Jíbaros and Hillbillies*, and a cofounder of the Affrilachian Poets, his poetry explores Black Puerto Rican identity, migration, memory, and the spiritual geographies of belonging. His was published in *The Louisville Review* and *Acentos Review* and others. He is a recipient of the Gilbert-Chappell Distinguished Poet Award for the Western Region of North Carolina.

* **Sabyasachi Roy** is an academic writer, poet, artist, and photographer. His poetry has appeared in *The Broken Spine, Stand, Poetry Salzburg Review, Dicey Brown, The Potomac,* and more. He contributes craft essays to *Authors Publish* and has a cover image in *Sanctuary Asia.* His oil paintings have been published in *The Hooghly Review.*

* **Santuella Kimani** is a writer from Kenya who enjoys interacting with the world through emotive art. She shares her works with a growing audience through her newsletter and Instagram page. She has recently delved into creating collage poetry, adding a visual element to her work. One of her poems, "The Reading" has been published by *Moonflake Press* in its latest issue, "Revival". She looks forward to continuing her adventure with words and evolving as an artist. https://thelightandthecracks.substack.com/.

* **Sarah Bradley** (she/her) is a Best of the Net nominee and an alumna of the American Short Fiction workshop; her stories have appeared in *Tahoma Literary Review, Flash Frog, Phoebe, 34 Orchard, Stanchion,* and *HAD,* among others. She lives in Austin, where she's working on a novel. Find more of her writing at www.sarahvbradley.com and follow her @sarahbooradley.

* **Shelby Newsom** is a queer, disabled poet and ecofeminist whose work explores themes of nature, embodiment, and resilience. She holds an MFA in poetry from Chatham University and helps indie authors, publishers, and literary magazines shape their work. Her poetry has been nominated for Best New Poets and appears in *Deep Wild, Flyway: Journal of Writing and Environment, Hawk & Whippoorwill, Parks & Points, Pilgrimage Magazine,* and *The Hopper.* Her debut chapbook is forthcoming in 2026 from *Gasher Press.*

* **Shui-yin Sharon Yam** (she/they) is a diasporic HongKonger currently residing in Kentucky. She is Professor of Writing, Rhetoric, and Digital Studies at the University of Kentucky.

* **Skyler Witherspoon** (they/them) is a genderfluid poet, digital artist, and freelance copy editor based in Portland, Oregon. Their poems have appeared in anthologies and magazines with *Train River Publishing, Sunday Mornings at the River, Doghouse Press,* and more. They are currently writing their first poetry collection. You can find Skyler's work on their Instagram @skylerwitherspoon.

* **Somrwita Guha** (she/her) is a poet and entrepreneur currently pursuing an MA in Creative Writing at the University of Lincoln. Her work explores postcolonial identity, memory, and migration. She is an editor at *The Lincoln Review* and recently hosted the Sloth Storytelling event at the Writers' Conference 2025. Guha has spoken at institutions including Presidency University, the University of New Mexico, and the Google Developers Meet. She is currently based in Lincolnshire, United Kingdom.

* **Sophie Pedersen** (she/her) is a Brooklyn-based poet who explores themes of desire, queerness, girlhood, and STDs in her writing. Sophie is an MFA candidate at NYU's Creative Writing Program, and her work has previously appeared in Lesbians Are Miracles and Black Warrior Review.

* **Stephanie Jones** (she/her) is a New York writer & poet with bylines in *The New York Times, DownBeat, NPR: Music, JazzTimes* and *The Detroit Free Press*. Her poems appear/are forthcoming in *Four Tulips, New Feathers Anthology, Orchards Poetry Journal, Eye to the Telescope, Entre: Magazine of the Arts, New Reader Magazine* & elsewhere, and as a commission for *Blue Note Records*.

* **Steven O. Young Jr.** (he/him) is knitted within the Great Lakes' mitten, where he earned an MA from Oakland University and occasionally slathers soundstages with his body weight's worth of paint. His latest literary homes include *Vita Poetica, Kind Writers, Rougarou, Chrysalism Press*, and *The Louisville Review*.

* **Taylor Kovach** (they/them) is a transgender poet residing in Riverview, Michigan. They hold an Honors Psychology BA from Michigan State University. One can peruse their work in *Nonbinary Review, Lavender Review, The Globe Review, Allium, Oddball Magazine, Belt Magazine, Literary Heist*, etc.

* **Taylor Necko** (she/her) has a BFA in Creative Writing from Bowling Green State University, where she served as Editor in Chief of Prairie Margins and wrote for Her Campus BGSU. Much of her creative work is focused on human relationships and how they transform. She has been published in *Gabby and Min's Literary Review, Route 7 Review, Periphery Journal, The Ear, Oakland Arts Review*, and *Midsummer Dream House*. Her publications are linked at https://linktr.ee/taylornecko.

* **Ty Zhang** (he/him) is a Thai-American writer and organizer. Originally from Rockford, Illinois, he is based in Albuquerque.. He writes poetry, prose, and screenplay. He is on Twitter at @khanombang. His work has recently appeared in *Assignment Literary Magazine, Progenitor Art & Literary Journal*, and *Meniscus*.

* **Zary Fekete** grew up in Hungary. He has a debut novella (Words on the Page) out with *DarkWinter Lit Press* and a short story collection (To Accept the Things I Cannot Change: Writing My Way Out of Addiction) out with *Creative Texts*. He enjoys books, podcasts, and many many many films. Twitter & IG: @ZaryFekete & Bluesky: zaryfekete.bsky.social